LUPE:

F. Eugene Barber

ISBN-13: 978-1508903536

ISBN-10: 1508903530

ACKNOWLEDGMENTS

I was urged by family and friends to write another murder mystery and although this is not really a murder mystery in the strictest sense, it is about murder.

I chose New York City as the initial setting for many reasons; it is a fascinating city; and it is the most diverse place I have ever been. Ethnicity doesn't mean much; the City is an American melting pot; Harlem, Spanish Harlem, The Village, Long Island, NY brownstones, Broadway, Manhattan, Brooklyn, Bronx, Flatbush, the waterfront, Queens; all different, but poured together as one. And Kings—Kings is rarely mentioned although there is such an entity.

I moved my character far away as I wanted her to start anew, and where better to start over than at the beginning of a new technology—Dayton—the birthplace of aviation.

I would like to thank Tom Mason for his editing of the final draft and early format suggestions. Mr. Mason owns and operates WordStyle Inc., a Las Vegas technical writing and editing firm.

And thanks to Cynthia Taylor for her blue-penciling. She lives in the city of Springs, Republic of South Africa, just an hour's drive east of Johannesburg. And Becky Hoff of Las Vegas took one last look; Thanks Becky.

Muchas gracias Maria Castillo I was enthralled by stories of your childhood before coming to the USA and becoming an exemplary citizen; I have been enriched just knowing you and I used a few pieces from your stories.

F. Eugene Barber
2015

Novels by F. Eugene Barber

ESCAPE: Along the Oregon Trail
SPOON VALLEY: Along the Santa Fe Trail
HOMESTEADING: Along the Mormon Trail
ABANDONED: Along the Grand Canyon
DEAD RINGER
DEAD RINGER #2
DEAD RINGER #3
WINDFALL
DEAD RINGER #4
BLAMELESS: No Way Out
THE FLYCATCHER
OUT OF THE DARK
Lt. Jack Taylor: An American Hero
CHI MEE: Émigré
NOT NECESSARILY MURDER
NEVER LOOK BACK
UNAUTHORIZED WITHDRAWAL
THE INTERLOPER: Terror Trains
LUPE: Street Smart

To be published soon:

CONFEDERATE GOLD
CHEROKEE SMITH: Trail Home
SODBUSTER: Trail to Nebraska
STUBBORN: Along the Spanish Trail
JUSTICE LIMPS
THE EXPERIMENT
WRONG PLACE
DEAD RINGER #5
SNIPER: One More Shot
RUNNING DRUMS
AMBUSH: Along the Chisholm Trail
BLIZZARD: Along the Sedo Trail
THE TRUCKERS
64 YEARS OF SECRETS (limited distribution)
VANISHED VACATION by Janet L. Morjoseph; edited by
F. Eugene Barber
LIVES (limited distribution)

CHAPTER ONE

The slim, blond girl ran as hard as she could. The alley was wet, dark, and there was a rank smell of decaying food—the strong smell of bad cantaloupe and old bananas. The last muffled gunshot still echoed. She could hear faint scrambling and slipping sounds behind her and a startled wet cat ran in front of her—the girl almost stumbled.

At the alley opening, she veered to the left, past the closed vegetable market, and headed for the bus stop. The rain had turned to mist. Her shoes slipped as she ran. She looked over her shoulder and saw a man running after her. If she timed it right, she would just make it; she forced longer strides as he waved his gun. Through the mist, she could see the turn signals weakly blinking on the bus. Her long legs were flying; she was taller than most Hispanic girls her age.

The first man slipped and fell. Lupe recognized him. She had seen him in the neighborhood near where her attic room was located. She kept running.

She turned her head back once again; two more men were running out of the alley. They stopped by the fallen man and then they spotted her nearing the bus. The two men darted around him. One of the men was holding a pistol. It had a long pipe silencer. He crammed it inside his jacket as he neared the street lamp and ran faster; his arms and legs pumping.

Lupe recognized him as well. She had seen him coming out of the liquor store near where she sometimes bought a cola. There were several, large wooden crates at the end of the alley behind the store. One crate, the smallest, she sometimes used for storing an extra pair of shoes or an old jacket. Perhaps he had seen her there.

Her attic room wasn't very large and she wasn't there much. Lupe had plans to rent a larger place as soon as she saved up enough money. She frequented this area often and was almost positive the fallen man had seen her and probably knew her name. She wouldn't come back here again for sure. She was frightened.

She had the correct amount of coins in her left hand. She had dug them out of her jacket pocket as she ran. The automatic doors were starting to close. She jumped! The bus left the stop. She was safe!

She peered out of the dirty, rain-splattered window. The three men had stopped on the far curb. One shook his fist at her; she ducked her head below the aluminum window edging. A truck drove between them going the other way. The bus gained speed. Lupe knew the fist-shaker too. She was breathing hard. She was not used to running so fast and besides she was both terrified and hungry; she had not eaten since early morning.

She looked overhead at the two broken lights above her seat. She thought, *I don't think they saw me very well. And the bus windows are smoked glass. They can't see me now.*

It was just wishful thinking. She began to doubt. She wasn't sure, *maybe they have seen me around the hotels. Or maybe they hadn't.*

She had frequented this section of the city several nights a week for the last six months. Her thoughts were churning and churning.

A few months ago Lupe had found that she could slip in through the back door of the hotel laundry room, late at night, and take a shower in the adjacent bathroom. Nobody ever knew. Sometimes if she crept in around three in the morning, she could wash and dry what few clothes she owned as well. She watched for the building guard even though he never checked the laundry room. The inside doors to the hotel kitchen were double locked.

The roving guard was usually on the top floors at that time of night. For some reason the door was never locked. It seemed broken. A person couldn't get into the hotel, only the laundry room and employee showers. The broken door was not noticeable. A person had to actually try the mechanism.

She had collected liquid soap bottles out of trash bins behind apartment buildings and carefully drained them. There was always enough soap left, a little in each plastic bottle for at least one washing. Lupe sometimes washed her clothes in the old cast iron bathtub on the third floor of her apartment building and then hung them on a line made of twine in her attic room.

She looked out through the bus window again and thought to herself, *perhaps they have seen me in the older section towards the river where I sometimes worked at a newsstand opening the newly dropped bundles of papers and magazines.*

She helped the owner open up in the early morning hour. He gave her five bucks each morning. On Saturday he let her pick an edition of a last week's magazine for herself. She usually picked up a travel magazine. She could always dream—a dream of getting off the streets and maybe even out of New York City. She didn't want to stay here the rest of her life.

The hotel tips were generally good. Lupe carried guest luggage from taxis and limos to or from the hotels. Lupe worked three of the larger hotels along the uptown street. Wall Street was just a few blocks away. The tips were often large. The regular bellhops didn't mind. The hotels were almost always short-handed.

She knew most of the bellhops that worked nights. Lupe had tried to hire in full time, but the hotels were only taking high school graduates; she had dropped out in the middle of her junior year. So she free-lanced and picked up what she could.

Lupe was really worried now. If she knew the three men, Lupe was sure they knew her. She sat quietly, finally gave up, and concluded, *the three men really do know who I am.*

She wished now that she had headed to her part of the city in a different way. She would not have seen them shoot the two homeless—their bodies were crumpled amongst the pasteboard boxes and trash.

Lupe Guzman was blond; she stood out; her hair color resembled a last-year's sheave of oat straw. She looked over the bus window ledge again. She could just barely see the men. They were running down the street to the south, towards some parked cars. The bus turned and they were out of sight. She supposed they had a car parked along the one-way street.

Lupe's worry turned to fright, *where can I go, it looks like they are going to follow me? I know, I can go, to my grandmother's in Spanish Harlem.*

She picked up a transfer slip from the slot as she stepped off and waited for the next bus going towards the river. She was lucky. The bus did not run often this time of night and it was just rounding the corner. Providence! Fate! Lupe crossed herself!

It was really raining now and the bus shelter leaked. Lupe jumped onto the bus quickly, before she became thoroughly wet, and before the three men found her. Her grandmother lived just a few blocks from the river in a run-down tenement. Lupe was sure she would be asleep at this hour. She wore a hearing aid, but not to bed.

Lupe hoped the door key was still hidden in the torn sheetmetal of the hallway heat return. She smiled wryly as she thought of the key's hiding place in the heat return grille, *heat indeed!*

The two rooms were almost freezing in wintertime. Her grandmother burned cheap candles to keep warm. Lupe's attic room was always warm; the heat from the other rooms rose. Her attic room was about a zigzag twenty blocks from the alley she had just left, *I better not go back to my attic room ever again. I don't have much there anyway. I don't even have any photographs or keepsakes, just old clothes.*

She looked out of the dripping back window of the bus again. She saw a shiny black sedan turn the corner. *Were the three men inside?* She watched it for three blocks. It finally turned off. Lupe gave a sigh of relief. She saw another bus shelter ahead.

She hopped off and waited for the next bus. If it didn't come soon, she would be forced to take a taxi although she could ill afford one. She was desperate. She knew that it crossed 96th and would eventually turn directly towards the river. She had taken this bus before to visit her grandmother. She looked at her Timex watch; the bus was eight minutes late. It finally came a few minutes later, still no shiny black car in sight.

Lupe repeated herself, *grandma's place is hot in the summer and cold in the winter. Heat indeed!*

The bus stopped and Lupe furtively looked behind her. It seemed to be clear; no shiny, black car was following. She ducked down an alley and came out in the middle of the next block. Lupe's grandmother's old tenement building was to the right. She waited in the dark for just a moment before venturing forth into the light. Her now stringy blond hair and shoulders were damp.

She was almost certain that the shiny, black car had kept going. But to be sure, she bent down behind the trash dumpster, hiding in the shadows, and then maneuvered her way in between the cars and trucks parked along the curb—staying low. The older style streetlight at the end was just a faint glow in the now steady rain.

There was a vibrating engine noise! She ducked down again. No shiny car; just an old Ford truck with a rusty looking refrigerator and two beat-up commercial washing machines in the back. It rattled on by.

Lupe breathed a sigh of relief. The hand-painted sign on the side said: Simón Appliances, *ah! I know him, Federico Jimonez.* She remembered him telling her that he used the ancient old-world meaning and spelling of his name on the sign—Simón.

She crossed the flooding asphalt, ducked into the building, and used the backstairs to the third floor. She felt for the key in the grille crack, it was still there—and opened her grandmother's door.

CHAPTER TWO

Rici Pantero swaggered into the bar. He was dressed in sharp looking, dark blue trousers, a fancy silk shirt, and a light, well-cut sports jacket. His shoes shined like glass. The shirt was open at the neck with the top two buttons un-fastened. Rici was cool! A heavy gold chain was around his neck. He wiped the wet toe of each shoe on his trouser legs above the half-inch cuff. The dampness didn't show on the dark blue cloth.

He peeled off a hundred-dollar bill from a roll and placed it on the bar and slid it forward, "Drinks for everyone my Man!"

The four men at the bar turned and smiled. They didn't know Rici or his name, but they had seen him around the streets. One man gave him a kind of two-fingered salute. He was missing a finger. The bartender poured them all a drink, including himself. Rici was pleased with the reception. They held their glasses high. Rici clinked the bartender's glass.

Earlier Rici had followed one of Scippio Ladero's men into an alley. The fellow hadn't heard him. Rici had knocked him on the head with a broken cement block and grabbed the bag that was secreted inside the man's coat. The man was not breathing; he had hit him too hard. Rici rolled the body in under some trash and threw several wet, sagging cardboard boxes on top.

He was nervous and scared, *man! Why did I hit him so hard?*

As he stepped out towards the alley front, Rici had wiped the soles of his shoes on an old carpet that had been shoved partly under a dumpster. He had looked down. They were still shiny and the decayed food was gone from the soles. There was a light mist in the air and it was starting to get colder.

Rici had been tracking the man's path for two weeks. He knew exactly what the man was doing and when to mug him. The guy was a 'collector' for Scippio.

Rici had moved quickly out of the alley and down the street, being careful. He was sure he had not been seen. He had turned the corner and sat on a partly broken, paint-peeled, bench by the stop and waited for the next bus.

He had looked inside the bag. It was crammed full of stiff packs of one hundred dollar bills. Rici had then carefully placed the money evenly into his inside jacket pockets and under his armpits inside the shirt. He had dropped the limp bag into a rubbish can by the bus stop. He felt his jacket, no lumps, nothing showed. He then buttoned his shirt and tucked it back inside his trousers. Some of the money slid down to his belt line. It still didn't show.

Rici caught the next bus back to the Eastside. He recognized his corner, and the blinking lights of the tavern, Rici hopped off the bus and went into the warm, inviting bar. Rici needed a drink. He was hyper—jittery. That night he was also feeling generous.

Antonio Chion took a sip of the free drink and said to himself, *I 'ave seen thees hombre before. Thees hombre does no 'ave thees kind of money to throw around. He done something bad.*

Tonio continued thinking...*if someone starts looking for an hombre, I could earn some serious dinero...*

Tonio waited at the far end of the bar, finished his drink, and then carefully followed Rici when he left, staying in the shadows. Tonio pulled on his earring while he followed. It must not be all gold; it hurt a little bit. *Damn street jeweler cheated me!* He would look for him tomorrow.

*Macio, you little father-less one...*quietly, but aloud, he cursed the street vendor in broken Spanish, French, and English.

Tonio's father was from Haiti and his mother was from Puerto Rico. Tonio didn't look like either parent. He could have passed for a cool guy from Little Italy. He knew, and sometimes he told the girls that his name was Tony.

He followed Rici for six blocks before he lost him! Tonio panicked! He ran towards the next corner.

Just in time! He spotted Rici going into the doorway of a walk-up flat in the next block. Tonio copied the address down on the palm of his hand with a cheap pen that he had stolen off the counter at the café down the street from the room he shared with his cousin Jaime Aragon.

He waited outside in the dark. Tonio soon saw a light go on inside a third floor window. He would listen to the street-talk and see who was interested. He wrote a '3' after the address.

CHAPTER THREE

Marti Fresno barged through the door and was blinded for a moment. He blinked; it was dark outside. There was a brand new streetlight just in front of the tavern, but it was not hooked up yet. The barroom entranceway was really bright. There were three hombres playing pool over in the far corner. Only an amber-shaded, hanging lamp lit the table's green felt. The three men were in its shadow. One had placed a five-dollar bill on the rail. It was his shot. He slowly dressed his cue tip with blue chalk.

Marti blinked again. His eyes adjusted. He wiggled his finger at his two compadres seated at the bar and pointed towards the rear. They swiftly followed him into the backroom, carrying their half-empty glasses. There was a table and five or six chairs. They played cards here a couple times a week. The three pulled up chairs; Manny sat on the left and Bernardo Garcia on the right.

"Patch didn't show! Something's happened. He's way late. He's supposed to be here an waiting for us."

They heard sirens. The three men jumped up from the table and looked outside through the rear door window. They couldn't see anything in the back alley. Red and blue lights were reflecting off the rear rooming house windows across the way.

The three men walked swiftly through the barroom and out into the street. Two cop cars were pulled up in front of the alley in the middle of the next block to the south. An emergency van was backing up next to the alley entrance. Its orange light was still rotating and flashing. A policeman with a camera had just finished. He had taken only two photos. They were not very interested. This was just another mugging.

The three men walked carefully in that direction. The 911 Emergency Crew was starting to bag a body, "Garcia, go check, see if it's Patch."

Garcia came back in a few minutes, "Si. It was Pancho, I mean Patch. He's dead. Mugged, the cops say. His wallet was gone, they said. I got there before they zipped him up."

"Ah! Abono! Patch was carrying over fifteen thousand. We got to get it back. I owe most of the dollars to The Man," Marti had once worked at a racetrack and had shoveled a lot of horse *abono* in his youth.

The three men waited near the mouth of the alley until the 911 crew and the police had left. The excitement was over and the small crowd had started to disperse; the sidewalks were soon empty. The three went deeper into the alley. The man who killed Patch might still be in the alley.

The cops hadn't looked. There was a scrambling sound in the rear and to the left, near the opening at the next block west. Manny fired at a shadow. There was a muffled scream to the right and Bernardo fired in the other direction. The shots were only a slight 'thump' sound. The homemade pipe silencers worked well.

The sound of running footsteps came from the eastern most mouth of the alley. Manny ran towards the street, slipped and fell on the wet roadway. Martin' Fresno stuck his gun under his jacket before he got to the streetlight.

Garcia was last; he glanced back at the two crumpled bodies. Then he saw the blond girl running towards the bus and quickly followed the rubia. The bus hissed air. The door closed and it took off into the wet night. He shook his fist at the bus. The rubia chica had gotten away. Their car was two blocks away and on a one-way street; going the wrong way.

"The *rubia* musta took our money! She saw us in the alley!" They put the word out on the street the next morning for a blond girl—a rubia chica.

Two days later Tonio approached Garcia, "Hey mon! You looking for an hombre that maybe 'offed' someone in an alley?"

"Si. Maybe."

"I might know something. What's it worth?"

"We'll take care of you Ho Kay. Whadda you know?"

"That night, a slick dude came into the bar, flashed a large roll of dinero, an bought us all drinks with a crisp one-hundred dollar bill."

"Do you know him?"

"No, but I got his address," Tonio hadn't washed his left hand for almost three days.

"Ho Kay! Two hundred if you are right an three hundred more if we find heem."

9

"Here's the address," Tonio held out his hand. Garcia, memorized it. He handed Tonio a small stack of twenties.

"Hola! If you know of a rubia about eighteen or nineteen—more for you," he waved a bunch of loose twenties as he walked away.

Antonio did know a blond girl. *I won't say anything yet. Maybe I can trade with her for something.*

He really didn't want to give them her name. Lupe always smiled at him when she saw him on the street. Tonio was not a bad looking guy and he knew it; most of the chicas liked him.

Garcia was talking to himself, *so the rubia didn't take our money. But she saw us and she heard the gunshots. She knows. Perhaps we can con this guy into thinking we know.*

He walked on down the street, thinking, *and I have seen her at the hotels grunting suitcases.* He thought to himself, *it was dumb for us to shoot the old man and the homeless woman.* They had panicked. No more mistakes—the three were cool now

CHAPTER FOUR

Lupe found the key. She stepped inside and silently closed and locked her grandmother's door behind her.

Lupe's grandmother had immigrated to America from Spain almost fifty years ago. She had married well, or so she had thought at the time. She had nice things, an apartment close to uptown, and they had a new car. Almost nobody in that part of the city owned a car.

Her new husband, Jorge Montero, always had money. He was a gambler, and seemed to be good at it, but then after a few years, he began to owe money. He couldn't pay. He had overextended himself and lost on the horses. The car was sold and then the lease on the nice flat was lost. Jorge had disappeared.

Ileana moved to Spanish Harlem and had gone to work. A neighbor lady tended their only child, Agostina, until she was old enough to go to school. Lupe's grandmother, Ileana, had lived in this two-room and a bath flat for as long as she could remember.

The police told Ileana that they figured the mob had buried her husband at sea or in a new building foundation. Back in those days, the mob intended for debts to be paid in one way or another.

Ileana Hirschmann Montero was blond and blue-eyed. And tall. Her father had been in the German Luftwaffe and had been assigned, by the Third Reich, as one of the pilots helping Generalissimo Franco's Spanish-African Army fight the Republicans against the Royals and Loyals. The pilot had fallen in love with the youngest daughter of one of Franco's staff officers and had married her in a full military ceremony on the second of February in 1938; Ileana was born almost ten months later. Her little brother was born the first week of November in 1940.

The Republican (Communist) anti-aircraft guns—40 mm Swedish Bofors, licensed to a munitions firm and made in England—had shot his Heinkel-111 down just before the ceasefire in March of 1939. The Civil War's end came on April 1st.

Major Ernst Hirschmann's body was never recovered. Ileana's mother was sure that some of the troops from the Abraham Lincoln Brigade or the Canadian, MacKenzie-Papineau Battalion (the Mac-Paps) had buried him in an unmarked grave in the dry hills of north central Spain—like so many others of the Luftwaffe and the few Italian planes that had crashed.

Near the end, the two Communist units had joined together and became the Internationalist 15th. Their combined war records were terrible; Ileana could find nothing about her father from their records that were filed in the military archives in Madrid. She had written numerous letters to the head of records and had received inconclusive notes from anonymous clerks.

As Ileana grew older, she had stopped inquiring officially. It didn't matter much, she had never been able to find out anything through regular channels, either through the US State department offices or in Spain.

Ileana's mother, Paola de Santos Hirschmann, had died shortly after the birth of her little brother. Something had gone wrong during the birth. Someday Ileana hoped to find him. She had looked for thirty-five years. The hospital had removed the boy when Paola died and placed him with an adoption agency. The aunt had no idea, and when she found out, it was too late—the papers were legally solid.

She had also written numerous letters, through the years, to orphanages and adoption agencies in Spain. Only one had answered. Her baby brother had been brought to them from the hospital and then given away and they didn't know who had raised him. Many records had been lost during a fire in 1962.

Ileana often wondered if he was still alive. She remembered that he had been named Karl rather than Carlos. And then one day, after thirty-five years, Ileana received a letter from an obscure records office in Madrid. Her hopes soared.

Ileana's aunt, Sofia Ybarra, had raised her. One day, an older, gray-haired man had arrived near the end of World War II and wanted to take Ileana back with him to Germany.

Ileana often thought of that time and sometimes talked to Lupe or to herself, *ah! Si. I remember him. Tia Sofia wouldn't let him in the front door.*

Ileana had watched from a window and saw him pace back and forth in front of their house. One day the older man brought a policeman to the door. Ileana's aunt Sofia still would not let them in. The policeman had asked her about the little boy, Karl, and about Ileana. The aunt didn't answer. She closed the door. Her aunt later wondered how the German knew about little Karl when she had not been able to find out anything herself.

Ileana had watched through the window and saw the policeman negatively shake his head and then walk away. After a week the older German man left his pacing and never came back. It was evident that there was no Spanish law that could help him.

Not long after that her aunt allowed Ileana to go back to school at the Church. She was in the second grade and would be promoted to third grade in a few weeks. Aunt Sofia had kept her at home when the man had first appeared. She was afraid he would steal her away. When Ileana was older, her aunt had told her that the gray-haired man was her grandfather Hirschmann. She didn't know his first name.

Guadalupe "Lupe" Paz Guzman looked almost exactly like her grandmother Ileana. They could have been sisters. Tall and straight, green eyes, flaxen hair, and the pale, peaches and cream complexion of an Aryan maiden. There was a slight difference— Lupe had almond shaped eyes.

Lupe had not acquired any of the darker DNA from her father or her mother. Her small, brown-haired, dark-eyed mother, Tina, had died of some frightful disease and her father, Gregorio, had been killed in a Greenwich Village alley. She remembered them both, but not well. Gregorio was from San Juan and had driven a taxi. Someone knifed him and had taken his taxi-fare proceeds for the night.

Only Lupe's teeth gave her a slightly Hispanic look; they long and white like Hillary Swank, the movie actress. Lupe's broad smile was pretty and her teeth seemed to fit her wide mouth— her gums didn't show when she smiled.

And her slightly Oriental shaped, hazel eyes, along with her high cheekbones, gave just a hint of her father's Arawak Indian ancestry. She was bordering on beautiful. Maybe with the right clothes and make-up she would be. Lupe didn't realize that she was beautiful; her only mirror was a storefront window glass.

Ileana was asleep in front of the television. Lupe tiptoed into the dark bedroom. She could barely see her grandmother's bed near the room's center, over in the corner was a small cot. Lupe curled up on the cot and was soon sound asleep. She had slept here many times before; it felt comfortable—and safe.

Ileana woke up after midnight, turned off the TV, and spotted her granddaughter—she smiled. The next morning Ileana woke Lupe up, "Lupita! Levántese! No mas sueño."

Lupe rubbed her eyes and laughed, "Ah! *Si abuela*. I am awake my grandmother."

"Why are you here young one?"

"I may be in trouble my *abuela*—my little grandmother."

"In what way Lupita?"

"I was walking by an alley last night where I should not have gone—yo tengo la culpa—I goofed. I should have gone a different way. I heard a muffled gunshot in the alley. I was behind the wooden crate where I store things sometimes and I was cleaning my shoes. I had just finished working at the hotels and I had stepped in some garbage crossing the curb ditch. It was misting and a little wet and cold and I was also having a hard time wiping the garbage away. I was leaning against the crate and the corner wall cleaning my shoes."

She stopped and looked up at her abuela, "Grandmother, a homeless man crawled out of a pasteboard box and fell flat. They had shot him. And then a woman in old clothes crawled out on the other side of the alley. They shot her as well. I think they thought those two persona were other people and perhaps had money. I hid for a moment and then ran for the bus stop when I saw it rounding the corner. The men chased me. I timed it just right. I know all three. Not their names, just by sight."

"You must go to the police Lupita!"

"No! Si. I would for sure be in much trouble. These people know things. They have friends in the police. They will find me and I too will be in an alley somewhere, covered in old boxes."

"You may stay here as long as it takes. I must go do trabajo now. I will be late for my work."

Lupe's grandmother worked at the laundry and dry-cleaners three blocks down the street. She had started there years and years ago, washing, starching, and pressing white shirts. Today it was mostly laundry; times had changed. Men no longer dressed in suits or wore ties. Casual was the 'in thing' for most companies not dealing with the public or foreign management and clients face-to-face. White shirts were almost outmoded.

Ileana had then operated the cash register for a few years and was now the assistant manager. Many things were automated in the shop. She was already eligible for Social Security, but she wanted to work a little longer. The plane ticket to Spain and hotels would take most of her savings. Ileana was not looking forward to retiring. She really liked to work. She knew everyone in the neighborhood. But she wanted to visit Spain before she was physically unable to do so. She was in splendid health; this was the time to go she had told Lupe a few months ago.

She often thought of her money hidden away. The travel idea had been much on her mind lately. Ileana often thought of her younger brother. She had been setting aside four dollars a week for years. She had never failed. The money was hidden in two coffee cans high on an open shelf in the small kitchen. Ever so often she would take out the ones and exchange them at the bank for twenties and the twenties for hundreds. There was over four thousand dollars in the cans.

If she watched the ads and found a special fare, she could fly to Spain and spend almost two months looking for her brother. The laundry and cleaners, where she worked, subscribed to a newspaper and she looked every day during her lunch break. Ileana had calculated the fare and costs many times. The American dollar was worth about seventy-five cents in Euro-dollars. She could do it! Spain no longer used pesetas, she had discovered.

Ileana remembered the trip to America so long ago. It had taken her almost three months to get the correct paperwork. She had ridden the train to Valencia. It had taken all day. The ship she had chosen was an old pre-World War II Greek freighter that had docked in Valencia harbor for repairs.

She had wangled a separate bunk, by saying that she would cook and clean for the officers on the way across the Atlantic if they would only let her come on board and be by herself. Even then the captain had extracted almost all of her pesetas from her, about two hundred dollars in US. She had another hundred dollars, in pesetas, hidden in her over-size shoes. She never took them off all the way across the Atlantic—except to change stockings.

The ship creaked and groaned constantly, even in calm seas. Ileana had been sick the first two days. After that, she was fine.

Flying would be so much better. She had never flown, but she had seen airplane movies on late night TV.

Ileana had started writing letters to Spain again. She had stopped for several years. She had received a last letter five years ago from the same obscure government records office in Madrid that had answered her before. It had contained a scantily worded note attached to poor copies of a birth certificate and an adoption notification.

The note had said that the Elazar Cados family had taken in her baby brother a year or so after the end of the war. They had called the boy Carlos Andre Meta Elazar Cados. She could not read the name of the village, but the state was clear, it was in the north, the copy was smudged, evidently from water damage to the original.

The clerk had written that there were no more records and suggested she check with the Church in her village. Ileana could not remember the name of the village and the birth confirmation was of no help. The clerk also mentioned that the name, Elazar, was a Basque given name and somewhat unusual. And he had said that perhaps they were French Basque or related anyhow—the name Andre hinted at that.

Ileana had left the village when she was six and had lived with her aunt Sofia in Madrid for eleven years. Her memory of the village name had faded, and she only vaguely remembered the surrounding geography.

She recalled some low hills to the west and she remembered that she could see the peaks of the Pyrenees to the north after her aunt had pointed them out. When covered in snow, they were beautiful, she remembered. Her wonderful Lupita had brought her a map of the Iberian Peninsula in Spanish.

Ileana had pored over the map night after night using a magnifying glass. She had finally narrowed the village location down to three places. The names did not really sound familiar; they just seemed to be in the right place. She picked the one closest to the northern border. The Basque and French given names, Elazar and Andre, were encouraging and caused her to pick a village near the French border deep into Basque Country and almost in France. She had waited over a year before she decided to write.

A few months later, after thinking about it, and just in case, Ileana wrote a letter to the Churches in the other two villages.

She did not know the names of the Churches; she just hoped the letters would make their way to the Padres.

The mail system in Spain was complicated. Often letters were sent to the wrong city. Sometimes one of her letters would be returned. She would mail it again and it seemed to go right through the system, she thought, *how strange.*

CHAPTER FIVE

Lupe ventured outside on the fifth day. She was afraid to go back to the hotel district or her attic room—she walked to the laundry. "Mia abuela. Do you need an extra persona to work here? I can do pressing. I would be *perdido* in t

Her grandmother was emphatic, "I don't want you working here. It is OK for a Spanish immigrant widow like me, you must do something better. And you would not be lost in back—we pull the curtain sometimes when it is hot in summer. "

"Maybe so, I need to make some money though."

"Lupita, you must go back to school. You can stay on the cot. We will be fine."

Ileana was thinking of her stash of money in the coffee cans, *perhaps I will not go to Spain for a while. Lupe is important. I would just have to work a year or so longer. I will be 68 soon.*

"Someday grandma. Someday. And soon! I am only nineteen. I have time. I need some money to live on and I cannot live off you and besides there is no room in your flat. It is too small. I know you say you do not mind, but it is *bueno* for only one."

Lupe walked back to the tenement and changed into some of her grandmother's older clothes. They were both the same size. She cut her long blond hair into a short, stylish, bob. She fluffed it a little and sprayed it with something from a generic can that her grandmother had on a shelf.

Lupe looked in the mirror. The clothes and the haircut made her look older. She wondered if she dared to go back to carrying suitcases again. She decided, *no, that is a bad idea.*

Lupe took a bus to Central Park. Her street friend Macio was usually there this time of day. He sold trinkets and souvenirs to the touristas.

He was there, "Hola! Macio! Selling anything?"

"Oh jes! This morning is good, a nice day. The *touristas* are out walking. *¿Que pasa?* "

"K-pasa yourself. A lot is happening. I may be in trouble on the street with Scippio's men. Can you find out?"

"Si. What are amigos for? Here, sell some of this stuff. I'll go for a walk and a bus ride and see. The prices are marked," he handed her his tray of merchandise. She strapped it around her neck.

A little over an hour later Macio came back. He had already heard that she was in trouble the day before, but he wanted to make sure and how much. He had been running hard, he was almost ill.

Breathlessly, "You gotta go! They know you. The word is out to look for a rubia named Lupe. They are offering money. Lupe, your rubia hair gave you away, you should stain it. Now just go!" She stood there, looking at him and took the scarf off here dark brown hair. He looked.

Macio took the tray and hurriedly left the park. He didn't want to be near her anyway.

Lupe yelled at him, "I sold a little Statue of Liberty! He didn't hear her.

"I'll pay him later. He didn't give me time to even say goodbye." She had made up her mind; she must hide.

She turned and headed towards the bus stop, she would catch one going to the west side. Perhaps she could go out around 72nd and stay a week or so. Scippo's men never came out that far. She knew of an alley.

As she walked, she thought about her situation. Lupe panicked. She had to get away. She stopped and looked around. Central Park was becoming crowded. New York was becoming crowded. The west end would do no good. She caught a bus and then transferred to one heading towards the eastside.

She thought of stopping at the Church for a few minutes before catching the next bus, "That is not a good idea. They might have someone there." Lupe crossed herself as the second bus passed the Church.

Lupe got off a few blocks from her grandmother's; stopped in a little variety store, and then walked to the flat. She unlocked the door. Her grandmother was still at work.

Lupe stripped off her sweater and short-sleeved blouse, *no sense in ruining my clothes with hair dye.*

She read the instructions on the box she had purchased at the store. The label said to remove all dirt, soap, oils, and hair conditioners. She washed her hair vigorously. She mixed and applied the liquid, using the thin, plastic glove inside the box.

19

An hour later she looked in the mirror. She jumped back, *I do not know myself. Now what shall I do? Or really, where shall I go?*

Lupe looked at the old telephone book, there was a map on the back, *New Jersey perhaps. Or out on Long Island, yeah! Si! Long Island or maybe Garden City. There are nice hotels in Garden City; I could carry baggage. I could catch the bus in Queens that would take me on the Big LIE; the 495 Long Island Expressway. I could be there in an hour or so. I could do a lot of stuff.*

She thought of Garden City, *ah! No! Scippio will find me eventually here in the East.*

I need to get further away than Long Island. She thumbed through the front pages of the phonebook. There was a long list of area codes. Lupe shut her eyes, turned the phonebook around and around and stabbed the pen. She looked at the chart printed next to the list. A city in Ohio had that area code.

Lupe believed in fate almost as strongly as she believed in God. She packed a few things that her grandmother had extra of, and wrote a long note in Spanish to her *abuela*. Most of the words were misspelled because she had never studied Spanish, only spoke it—New York style. At the bottom she instructed her grandmother to burn the note. She was afraid to go back to her attic room. There was not much of value there anyway. She counted her money. She had forty-seven dollars and change. She 'borrowed' some money from her grandmother's coffee cans for the bus ticket. She added the amount to the note. As she left, she stuck the door key back into the crack of the sheetmetal grille cover, *I might be back someday.*

CHAPTER SIX

Rici had decided not to hide the money in his room. He didn't trust the landlord. He made a special carrier out of an old cloth and tied it around his waste. He walked outside; the bulge wasn't noticeable. He had spent some of it and had sent some of the money to his mother in Puerto Rico—almost a thousand dollars. He had spread the bills between two pieces of cardboard and had mailed them in a large envelope lined with bubble pack.

He needed a drink. He headed for a bar four blocks north. The bar was packed, "I'll go across the street."

He looked around as he crossed, *I think I'm being followed,* he didn't like it and figured something was wrong. Rici knew that he had not been seen in the alley the other night, *how have they found out about me? Or have they?*

Rici ducked around the corner instead of going inside and watch. In a few moments a heavy-set man rounded the far corner. Rici peeked from behind the brick façade, *I know of him. He is one of Ladero's.*

He repeated himself, *how have they found this about me?*

Rici ran through the alley and down the block, he ducked into another dark and damp alley, *I've messed up,* he realized too late that it was a dead end. It was too narrow for big trucks and wasn't used much.

The heavy-set man turned into the alley after him. It was Garcia. "Give me the money Rici," his hand was inside his jacket pocket, there was a definite bulge; his open left hand was outstretched.

A gun maybe? A knife? Rici wasn't sure. He reached carefully into his new jacket and brought out several bundles still wrapped in the cloth.

He untied the cloth and handed the bills over, "How did you know?"

"Because you are *estupido* Rici. You spent our money."

A flash of steel; Rici had a surprised look on his face and slumped towards the ground. He watched his fine silk shirt slowly becoming blotched with a red stain. Rici wondered, *how will I ever clean it*, as the darkness came over him?

Garcia wiped his knife on Rici's new jacket and walked slowly away. He quickly counted the money, there was just a little over ten thousand, "Skippio will be upset," he said to nobody in particular.

An hour later a bag lady, pushing her rusty, over-flowing, grocery cart down the alley, saw the body. She told the storekeeper.

A few minutes later a patrol car pulled into the alley, sirens silent. The The two policemen talked to the bag lady.

She had seen nothing; "I come here at this time every day. I look for things to sell and things that the store throws out. Sometimes I find something good to eat. Yesterday it was an old, dry chocolate cake. The inside was real good," she smacked her cracked lips—a hairy mole was near one corner.

She turned away and pushed her shopping cart on down the alley towards the far sidewalk. The now silent emergency van pulled up behind the patrol car.

"Sergeant. I know this one. He did hang out in Spanish Harlem and took book. He was sometimes a runner for Ladero and he was also a part time mule; he transported drugs for Ladero. His name's Rici Pantero. Ricardo actually. We have picked him up for questioning a few times and we did find a needle set once, but nothing ever stuck. Pardon the pun," he chuckled under his breath at his own humor.

Timothy Cullen, a burly Irish sergeant, originally from the Bronx, nodded, "That's four bodies we've found this week. What's going on?" Tim pushed the thick, red hair out of his eyes and wrote something in a small notebook. His grandfather had been a cop and his father still was.

The other officer said, "I don't know. We need witnesses for some of these. We can put the word out. Maybe some of the street snitches will know something."

They did; two days later a wisp of a girl climbed up the steps of the precinct office. She looked out into the street behind her and ducked quickly inside.

The front desk officer, Eddie Kirkpatrick, saw her, "Hi Millie! Long time no see," he dropped his pencil on the desk and looked up at her through the opening in the iron barred front window.

"I have something to say, is Mr. Jimmy in his office?'

"Yeah! He's back there. I'll buzz him."

Lieutenant Jimmy Fagan escorted Millie inside and they sat at a paint-chipped table just outside his office.

"The street is looking for a blond girl."

"Oh! Who's lookin' and who's the girl?" This was the first time the Lieutenant had heard anything about it. He had twelve cases going.

"It is a gang. Ladero's people. She is called Lupe, Mr. Jimmy. I don't know her last name. She works at the hotels sometimes. I have seen her there. I work there sometimes in housekeeping as a fill in."

"What do you suppose she saw?"

"The street says she saw a shooting."

"We need to find her before they do then."

He opened his desk, "OK Millie. Here are some food stamps. I can't give you much else. Take them to Paco's Market. He understands. And thank you. We'll follow up on this and find her."

"Oh! Thank you Mr. Jimmy. These will help my mother. And I hope you find her before they do."

The Lieutenant was careful not to overburden Paco with "contributions." Jimmy only used the food stamps once a month. He sometimes waited a week or two longer. Ever so often he would take up a collection in the office. He would just walk around with an open envelope; they all knew what the charity was. The collection was never much, but it helped Paco.

The Lieutenant couldn't help but like Millie. She seemed so helpless sometimes. And she had never been in any kind of trouble although she was from a rough neighborhood and had some pretty rough friends or perhaps acquaintances was a better word. He doubted if they were really friends.

Millie was part Black and part Irish. She was intelligent and earned money by doing odd jobs in the smaller hotels that couldn't afford full time help. Millie fit the bill. The managers liked her and she didn't want a forty-hour job right now as she went part time to New York City College.

She slept on the pullout couch in the three room flat with her younger sister Laytha. Their two brothers slept in the living room on an old couch. Laytha was at an impressionable age, but Millie was working hard to keep her focused on high school and a few decent friends. Their mother worked nights as a cleaning lady in one of the city buildings.

Millie had no idea where their father was. He had left when she was nine—California perhaps. Her mother thought so. Her cousin had been in Los Angeles working and thought he had seen him in Compton.

Paco Lero did understand. This was Paco's contribution to his community. He recycled the thirty dollars worth of food stamps back to the precinct to be used again and again. He appreciated the collection envelope when it came, although he didn't expect it.

Sometimes when the recipient came into the store with these special stamps, he threw in an extra something—an orange or a couple of apples. Paco's Korean wife scolded him every time he did. He did it anyway, hopefully when she wasn't looking.

CHAPTER SEVEN

Lupe carefully stepped off the bus. Her left leg had gone to sleep during the last fifty miles of the long ride. The bus seat only tilted back a couple of inches and she had slept fitfully. She had been leaning her head against the cold, metal window ledge. She had finally waded a sweatshirt up and rested against that for a while. The jolting and vibrating of the bus had still kept her awake most of the way.

She was carrying an old army duffel bag—a leftover from the Gulf War. Someone had thrown it away and it was stamped: CPL H E Schmidt. There was a small hole cut in the heavy material where the social security ID number had been. Ft. Riley - Kansas was ink-stamped below the unit numbers. She had sewn and patched a long tear in the bottom. It was serviceable.

Lupe looked around the bus station. On an outside wall there was a faded city map mounted inside a poorly painted pine frame and covered with clear plastic. She looked at the leyenda. It gave the bus station address—leaking rainwater had blurred the rest of the legend, that listed the address and phone numbers of the Police Department, Fire Department, City offices, etc. They were unreadable. Near the bottom edge of the city map there was an orange star and a caption:

YOU ARE HERE

The border was framed in hotel and motel ads. She knew she could afford none of them. She looked across the street and then down the block towards the east. There were two sets of train tracks and she could see some older buildings in the distance on the far side. Most of them had peeling paint, dirty windows, and plywood pieces had been stuck into the frames of a few broken windows.

Lupe looked around the bus station, *perhaps I can sit here for the rest of the night.* The seats were dirty and most were slit. Black duct tape patched three or four of them, however most of the cuts in the material were untouched, they were left to disintegrate even more.

In the corner was an old man in rumpled clothing. He was constantly hacking and clearing his throat, while sucking on a cigarette. A young woman, sitting over in the corner by the vending machines, was nursing a small baby. She had a broken suitcase and two plastic grocery bags, stuffed full, sitting at her feet. An old leather belt held the suitcase together. The leather belt had once belonged to a big man.

The young woman kept looking at the door and slumping as if trying to hide. Lupe figured she was running from something or someone—perhaps an abusive husband. There was a bluish bruise on her temple. She had tried to cover it with heavy make-up. Lupe wondered if the large belt had belonged to her husband. She wasn't wearing a wedding band, perhaps an abusive boyfriend.

A fat man, with two sample cases, sat by the window near the door. He got up and moved outside, he had an unlit cigar in his mouth. His lighter was in his left hand. An elderly couple sat across from him. The old man was nodding and jerking his head in his sleep. He woke himself up and dozed off three times while Lupe was looking around.

The only decent seat was by the heater fan. It was very noisy because a blade was bent and out of balance. Lupe went outside through the second set of double doors that were being propped open by two orange, plastic street cones. She started walking.

An hour later she was peering out through one of those dirty glass windows on the third floor of the building she had spotted when she stepped off the bus.

So this is Dayton. She looked towards some tall, far-off buildings, *I need to find work. Maybe up that way.* She saw a Wright-Patterson AFB sign near a two-lane highway leading eastwards towards Harshman Ave.

Lupe slept fitfully. Her empty stomach growled. The Conrail tracks were less than a half-block away and railroad work cars had moved back and forth from midnight until almost time to get up. There were several workmen doing something to the tracks and road bed; around the clock it seemed. They turned the floodlights off just as she walked outside. The low hills to the east were pink. The morning sun was just breaking through the low clouds. It smelled like it might rain.

She grabbed a newspaper from a "trust me" rack sitting outside the small café. Lupe slipped out the two pages of want ads and stuck the rest of the paper back inside the rack cover. Most people didn't read the want ads anyway. She could have probably dug the ads out of the nearby trash barrel, but she didn't feel like it. She remembered the hacking old man at the bus station.

Lupe stepped inside and ordered a cup of coffee and a muffin. The waitress was busy. Lupe emptied the contents of four little Knott's Berry Farm jelly boxes onto her muffin. She dumped three creams into her coffee along with three scoops of sugar. She was hungry. Her last meal had been in New York. The calories would be needed.

She ate the muffin hurriedly, before the waitress came back, and then gulped down the last of the coffee. She left a dollar eighty on the counter top with a fifteen cent tip. Even though small, she knew what tips meant to a person.

Three hours later she had a job cleaning restrooms, floors, and hallways in a downtown hotel. They gave her a mop, broom, rags, a big, plastic trashcan on wheels, spray bottles, and two pair of rubberized cotton gloves. They were stiff and looked as if they had been dipped into the rubber material. She was paid fifty cents over minimum wage and was allowed a free lunch, but she could only eat leftovers after the noon rush was over and she had to eat in the back part of the kitchen.

The cooks had set up an old card table. They sometimes drank coffee there on their break between breakfast and lunch. She could eat there, they told her. Lupe was pleased, *I can hide here in Dayton for as long as it took.*

CHAPTER EIGHT

Central Park was crowded. The two policemen spotted Macio and his tray of goods. One held out his badge. "We are looking for a blond girl about your age. Probably Latino. Have you seen anyone like that around here? We believe that her first name is Lupe."

Macio moved his eyes back and forth and said, "No, I do not know any blond Latinos." They knew he was lying.

He sat his tray of trinkets on the bench beside him and looked up at the two tall policemen. Cops always intimidated Macio. They noticed!

"Look man. If you know something you better tell us. We'll have to run you out of the park. You don't have a vendor's license."

Macio thought for a moment. "OK. Si! Her name is Lupe Guzman. I do not know where she is. She is gone. I have not seen her for more than two weeks. She was running from Scippio Ladero's men," Macio was upset and visibly shaking. "They will keel her if they find Lupe."

"Alright Macio. You can stick around. Don't short change any touristas or we will come back and run you in."

"No man. I am honest," he was starting to feel better. He had hated to tell them Lupe's name, but he had to make a living. Things were tough on the street.

Tonio had been watching from a distance and saw the two policemen. He decided it was not a good time to confront Macio about the phony gold-plated earring. He had trashed them yesterday; his lobes had turned green. He left.

Two days later, the two officers knocked on Ileana's door, "Ma'am. We are looking for your granddaughter, Lupe Guzman. Do you know where she is?"

One held his ID card and badge out for Ileana to see, he looked into the plain, but clean room. The furniture was old, well worn, but serviceable.

Ileana was a little frightened. She clutched an odd-sized envelope, with a foreign stamp in the corner, to her chest as she spoke. In her left hand was a piece of lined, yellow paper torn out of a tablet.

"I do not know for sure. She left me this note," she had not burned it as Lupe had asked.

Jimmy could read Spanish, "So she has gone out of state. Any ideas where?"

"No! The old phone book was on the table and it was open to a page; this one."

The two policemen looked at the page—Area Codes. There was a pen prick next to three of the numbers.

"Lupe must have done that. She believes in los Sinos....excuse me....The Fates."

"I know of los Sinos. Do you have a photograph? We'll bring it back."

"Si. Here is one. I'll take it from the frame for you." She didn't hesitate, she was fearful of the police.

"Ok. Thank you. If you hear from her, you must tell us. Here is our phone number," he gave her a card and handed her fifty cents to call with; he had noticed there was no working phone. The phone plug was disconnected from the wall plate, *she probably can't afford a phone,* he thought to himself.

They left to drive back to the precinct. He drove carefully back to the station, "Look up area code 937; it had a line under it, and then look up the other two."

The younger policeman grabbed a book and thumbed through the new phonebook, "It's Dayton, Ohio. Shall I notify the local police?"

"Sure. We need her as a witness. And list her as a flight risk on the Form. We'll think of something else for them to arrest her for as well. Dayton eh. Man, that is a big area. We got our work cut out for us. Must be a million people in area code 937. And who knows, she may still be here in New York or she may have gone to the other two."

The young officer had looked up the other two. "One is Topeka and the other is Oklahoma City."

Within two hours an all points bulletin, with Lupe's photo, had been distributed to every law agency around Dayton including the Sheriff's Office in surrounding Montgomery County.

Computers and email were wonderful. They were bound to find Lupe sooner or later. A very wide net was being thrown.

After the men had left, Ileana looked again at the new letter from Spain. It was from the Padre of the Church in Villa Belon just north of Segovia and just a couple of kilometers off the road to Valladolid—an ancient city. She had found them all on the map. This was not as far north as she had thought.

The Padre was delighted to get her letter. He had never received a letter from America before. He wrote that indeed there were many Cados family members buried in the Church cemetery and that there was an Enrique Elazar Cados buried there. The dates on the stone would be about right. This could be her little brother's adoptive father.

Enrique Elazar Cados had died in 1969. The original Padre that had presided over the funeral had been replaced and then replaced again. The present Padre had only been there a few years. He did not know of the family, but he wrote that he would ask around and write her again. He had also written that Elazar was an uncommon Basque given name.

Lupe walked slowly back to her room. It was getting dark. The streets were beginning to fill with 'night' people. The Conrail tracks were to her left and the Findley Street sidewalks were becoming crowded. She was alert and watching the side streets and the alleys.

She had a few blocks to go. This part of Dayton was a little scary. Lupe thought for just a moment, that she was back in a bad part of New York City. She turned left and started walking towards East 3rd. A drunk staggered in front of her and stopped. Lupe ducked around him and ran!

She ran fast and was soon in the apartment compound and then inside her rented room. Nobody had been behind her. She used the steel, oddly shaped key, and unlocked her door. Somebody had been inside—probably the landlord. She was used to that. Her attic room had often been intruded by the landlord while she was gone.

Her few clothes had been moved and one drawer in the wooden chest had not been closed all the way. She knew she had closed it tightly when she left. She propped a tall-backed wooden chair against the oval shaped, glass doorknob; the only chair in the room.

Lupe washed her face and hands and crashed on the bed. She had gorged herself on leftovers at lunchtime. It was to be her only meal. She was tired. An hour later her eyes came slowly open. There was a slight noise coming from somewhere. In the reddish glow, coming from the sign on the building front across the street, she could see the oval doorknob turning.

Lupe quietly picked up the broom left behind by the last lodger. A hand slipped around through the crack and moved the chair ever so slightly, she turned the broom around and came down hard on the wrist and flipped on the light.

It was the drunk—only he wasn't drunk. She hit his wrist again through the three-inch crack and then poked at him in the face with the handle end. He retreated slowly and then ran when several doors along the hallway started opening.

He was definitely not drunk.

Lupe shook her head, *I must find a better place.* She tilted the wooden chair back against the doorknob and stomped the two legs into the old green, shag carpet. Lupe was really tired, *the long trip and stress did that I suppose.*

She was soon sound asleep again.

CHAPTER NINE

Officer Thomas Delano was seated on a hotel lobby bench. He had been watching the people in the lobby for an hour. The sergeant had assigned him here two weeks ago, knowing that the girl had worked in hotels in New York, carrying baggage.

He looked at the photograph. Then he looked up at the girl scrubbing the marble pillar by the lobby desk. She was polishing off a long collection of fingerprints and smears. He and his partner had been looking for three days. Tom took his pen and darkened in the hair of the girl in the photograph. She was Lupe.

Tom had been on the police force over three years. He had gone to college for two years, getting an AS in police science and he was still going to night school one night a week; taking Criminal Justice—Thursdays. That was his day off. He worked on Saturday and got most Sunday's off. He had been an apt partner and a quick study under the old sergeant who told stories while sitting in the driver's seat of the waiting police van. The stories all had a point to them.

From the patrol van, the sergeant was watching the sidewalks in front of the other two hotels—Delano had a radio and kept in constant contact with the sergeant. The Lieutenant had put both the sergeant and Tom Delano on plain-clothes duty last March.

The flyer said the girl was a flight risk. He hadn't been told exactly why she was wanted in New York, but it didn't matter. There would be a new printout soon and he could pick it up from the patrol van's micro-printer.

Tom walked over and quickly slapped a nylon quick-cuff on Lupe's wrist and stuck his badge in front of her nose, all at the same time. She jumped and jerked back. He held her steady.

"Are you Lupe Guzman from New York City?" He knew she was.

"No! I am Sally Lindstrum and I live here in Dayton."

"Then you won't mind coming along with me. We'll just walk slowly out towards the unmarked van out front. We don't need to attract any attention. Take your gloves off very carefully and drop them on your cart. Leave the cart just as it sits."

He gently pulled her along, attached to the nylon strap, as he headed for the van. He slid the door open. She was tall and this was a mini-van. He pushed her head down under the door opening and sat her in the backseat. He slid in beside her and attached the other end of the nylon to a bar made for that purpose. It had an elongated slot.

He moved up front. Delano's partner, Sergeant Mike Strand, started the van and then quickly drove away. There was a heavy gauge wire, folding screen between the front and back seats. Tom slid it on its runners between the front and back seats and latched it from the front. There were no inside handles and no door locks.

Tom turned towards the backseat as Mike drove carefully down Wayne Avenue, "The entire police force and half of the deputies in Montgomery County are looking for you." He held up her picture with the inked hair, "I'll read you your rights... you have the right to remain silent and you have the right to...."

He droned on and Lupe just nodded. She was numb. She was sure Scippio Ladero's men would find her now.

"Alright. Si! So I am Lupe. Why is it that you are seeking me here in Ohio?"

Mike thought her slight accent was cute, "We aren't. It's New York City. They want you,"

Delano thought she was cute too, not just her accent—she was very pretty actually.

"For why? I have done nothing."

Delano turned the second sheet of the stapled flyer over and read the back for the first time, "They say you saw the killers of an old man and a homeless woman."

"I know nothing. What will you do with me?"

"We are sending you back to New York."

"But the Ladero men will find me! That is why I left. The police will find me dead in an alley."

"You will be protected well I am sure. We always protect a witness here in Ohio. I am sure they will do the same in New York City."

He checked in. There was an earpiece in his ear. He turned, "They will have tickets waiting for us at the train station. I'm taking you to New York City in the morning. The Lieutenant just informed me. I'm off duty in an hour and you will placed in a special holding room. It is clean and the cot is not bad. I have slept on it myself when I pulled a long shift and didn't feel like driving home. I'm single and I don't even have a fish or a cat."

Thomas and the Sergeant took her inside and turned her over to the officer waiting for them.

Tom said, "I'll see you in the morning Miss Guzman."

She didn't say anything. She just glared at the guard. The guard took her to the room that the cot was in and locked the iron barred door. The little room was all by itself and had a restroom.

"We stop here for twenty minutes folks. You may get off the train and stretch your legs. Just don't stray. I'll be re-boarding everyone shortly," he proceeded on down the aisle, repeating his announcement over and over. He moved to the other passenger car. Several people got off and were looking around the station platform.

The fellow thought the train business was tough. When he wasn't going up and down the aisles, he helped out in the dining car. His father had been a conductor and had complete authority —not that way anymore. He sometimes even resorted to serving meals when someone was ill.

He shook his head and wrote something on a clipboard. He had been working for the railroad longer than his father, who was now retired. He felt like a pawn sometimes. He wondered how long it would be before they automated his job.

Tom rose and pulled Lupe up carefully. He had wrapped his handkerchief around the handcuff. It had been chaffing her, "We won't go outside. We'll just walk up and down the aisle a little. Most of the passengers are used to us by now, but we'll stay inside. Once we start moving, I'll slip the cuffs off again."

They both worked out the kinks—they had been on the train since four in the morning, Dayton time.

They were on their sixth traverse of the car when the diesel train engine started making grunting noises. The same man was hurrying everyone back on board.

"C'mon folks! Time to climb aboard. This is our second to last stop," the passenger cars soon filled back up. Thomas and Lupe took their seats.

"Lupe, I almost hate to see this trip end. I have really enjoyed talking to you."

"Me too! Maybe under different circumstances..."

The train jolted to a start and slowly gained momentum. The green grass, trees, and fence posts were soon whizzing by.

Tom looked at her, "How did you get the name Lupe?"

"From Saint Guadalupe, I was named after the Saint and the town in Spain where Saint Guadalupe first appeared over six hundred years ago. My grandmother had made a pilgrimage to the town when she was a young girl. My mother remembered hearing the story and named me because of the story. She calls me Lupita—little Lupe."

She looked out of the window at the whizzing scenery for a moment, "Our Lady of Guadalupe appeared again in Mexico, to a Christian Indian, and used the Aztec Nahuatl word of Coatlaxopeuh as her name. This Indian word is pronounced "quatlasupe" and sounds remarkably like the Spanish word Guadalupe."

"They named the town Guadalupe, but it was changed to Madero over seventy-five years ago. A part of a man's full name actually—I forget all of it—I worked with a few Mexicans in New York and I asked them about my name."

The train was going by the north side of some low hills and the sun was blocked out for a few moments. She started talking again when they were back into the sunlight, "I also know these things are true because I looked up my name in the encyclopedia of my *abuela*. My grandmother bought them for a few dollars when I was small. She said I would need them someday. The books are almost twenty years old."

"I was named after St. Thomas."

Lupe looked up from her seat, "You are Catholic like me?"

"Yep! Don't always go to Mass, but I manage to at least talk to the Father when my duties take me in the area. Some of my ancestors were from southern France."

"It did not come up in our conversation."

They were quiet for the next few miles. Each thinking. The clickity-clack sound of the wheels was both boring and mesmerizing. Lupe leaned her head against Tom's shoulder. She wasn't aware. She was fast asleep.

They had talked and talked, almost all the way from Ohio. They had talked of living on the street in New York, being street smart, school, her grandmother, his grandparents, and the little farm just outside of Dayton that he had grown up on. And the two murders she had witnessed—well witnessed the men running out of the dead-end alley.

His maternal grandmother and grandfather had reared him when his parents had been killed in a head-on collision. He was only ten—he missed them still. Thomas loved his grandparents, but there was something missing. He had often wished for a brother or a sister. As he grew older Thomas knew that was impossible, he was all alone!

Thomas smelled Lupe's hair. There was just a hint of a dye smell. He smiled and said again to himself, "She is really very pretty." He wondered what she would look like as a blond. He carefully fished her photo out of his inside jacket pocket and wished he had not darkened in her hair. Tom found that he liked her. She didn't move—she was in a deep sleep.

I will find another flyer back at the office. Or better yet, it was probably on the police LAN in JPEG. He figured he could print out a wallet size, on good, glossy paper. He chastised himself for being juvenile. He would never see her again. He dozed off too. Leaning together, the pair looked like special friends or sweethearts.

The train was slowing down. It awakened him, Tom looked at his watch, less than twenty minutes before they arrived. An unmarked police car was supposed to be waiting for them. He set his watch to Eastern Standard Time. He gently shook Lupe awake.

"Would you like to wash your face?"

"OK, Si. Yes."

Delano escorted her to the front and unlocked the handcuffs he had put back on Lupe before they arrived at the station. He waited outside the narrow door. He slipped the cuff from his own wrist and waited by the windows.

When Lupe came out, he slipped the handcuffs back on, "I only put these on for show. They are not very tight. I don't want the NYPD to think we are hicks back in Ohio."

She nodded and smiled. He placed his handkerchief into the cuff again, it was chaffing her wrist even when it was loose. The cuff didn't bother him, he had on long sleeves.

The ride from the station to the precinct was slow. They had arrived when the traffic was at its worst. Tom had never been to New York City before and noticed right away that it was not spread out like Dayton. He supposed real estate was expensive and that they utilized every square foot.

The car pulled up in front of an old building with steep steps. The two were escorted through the swinging gate and inside the first big room. Tom took off the cuffs and retrieved his handkerchief, "I'm sorry I had to do this. You were considered a flight risk by the NY police." He said it loud enough for the office staff to hear.

She grinned and said softly, almost whispering, "I was planning to take off at the first chance. But because of you, I decided to stay."

She continued and still whispering, "I watched for every opportunity to skip, until I started talking with you. I enjoyed the train ride."

A big, burley cop, led Lupe away, she turned and waved just as they went through a double-door.

Tom turned to the sergeant, "Give me a ride back to the train station please. I'll sleep on the train. I wanta get back to Ohio."

He didn't like the Big Apple.

Too many people.

CHAPTER TEN

Lupe was frightened. They had talked to her for three hours. The police had tape recorded everything. She felt as if they thought that she was somehow involved.

Finally the older balding cop in a three-piece suit let up, "We're sending you home now; to your grandmother's. Don't leave town though. You are not under arrest, but we could do that. And we'll have a patrol car circle the area every hour or so. It'll be at random so don't be alarmed if you don't always see one."

"Oh by the way. We will be arresting Scippio Ladero and two of his hoods one day this week, maybe Friday. It takes paperwork. We won't be able to hold Scippio very long, but we love to harass him when we get the chance. Lupe, from what you have told us, we can hold two of his scum-bags for indictment and trail."

Lupe looked at him, "That will be good. I am afraid of them all." She couldn't remember the last time she had seen anyone in a three-piece suit, even at the hotels.

"Yeah! We'll have a line-up and bring you in to identify them. We can't find the third one, but we're looking. We also have the three affidavits you signed," he held them up and placed them in a folder, "I made copies and sent them to the prosecutor's office. He asked for them. He has been after Ladero for years."

Lupe was still frightened. She believed Scippio Ladero would find her in spite of the patrol cars. The two policemen dropped her off down the block from her grandmother's flat. It was better that way. She ducked into the alley and came into the building the back way. She found the secret key.

She pulled down the cheap, discolored blinds and turned on the black and white TV. She tweaked the rabbit ears and watched the early news on a local station. The female Senator from New York was speaking. She listened for a moment, became bored and switched the channel to a cooking show on NBC.

My grandmother says next year she will have to buy a conversion device—television would no longer be transmitted in the same manner. It was a government subsidized device.

A young lady was preparing some kind of French dish. She would rather watch Martha Stewart—she was sloppy—pieces of dropped and splattered food was all over the set. Lupe usually watched TV in the window of a department store downtown or in one of the hotel lobbies between carrying bags from taxis and limos.

Lupe liked the soaps. She only saw them once in awhile. Usually she could figure out what had gone on even though she had missed several episodes. She turned the cooking show off and switched to a game show replay.

She dug out the "D" encyclopedia from her grandmother's small collection of books and looked up Dayton. It wasn't there. She pulled "O" and found Ohio. There was a half column on Dayton. It wasn't too enlightening. Lupe flipped to the front of the volume—the date was 1961, "No wonder," she said aloud, "I had forgotten how old these really were."

She was still thinking of running away again. She liked Dayton. Perhaps she was thinking of Tom. If she ran, she would live in a different part of the city.

In Dayton, she had noticed a sign pointing to Wright-Patterson AFB, "Maybe there will be some work out that way. A café perhaps, soldiers like to eat away from the Base." All servicemen were either soldiers or sailors to Lupe. She needed to know more about Dayton.

Ah! The internet.

She could go to the library and wait for a turn at the computer. There were four computer stations at the small library twelve blocks away. The stations were almost always full. Nobody in this part of the city could afford to buy a computer and the local library was the only source. She wasn't real good at it, but she could get by. She used OPERA as a search engine. GOOGLE was ok, but gave her more than she was looking for most of the time.

Lupe had learned how to use a computer in school. She often wished she could have stayed and finished. It had been almost two years now. There was just not enough money. Her grandmother only had a few pennies left each week after everything was paid for and they had purchased food. AND her grandmother must put away the four dollars. That was a ritual she could never disturb, *I can always go to Queens. The library there has more computers and they are not always so busy. When I get a good job and settled somewhere, I'm going back to school.*

The knob was turning on the door. She waited. Hardly breathing. It reminded her of Dayton. Her grandmother's head popped in. She was startled for just a moment.

"Hola! Abuela Ileana. I'm back. For a little while anyway."

Her grandmother gave her a big hug and a kiss.

CHAPTER ELEVEN

Tom drove the patrol car towards a secluded spot near the RR tracks. He was looking for a perp that pretended to be a drunk. The man had attacked and beat up three women in the last several months, both within a mile of Washington Park. He hadn't raped them—just beat them up and had then taken their purses. The man hated women in a different way than traditional rapists, the police psychological profiler, Dr. Brecht, had said.

Lupe had given Tom a very good description while they were riding the train. He pulled in under the island cover of an abandoned, old style, filling station. The roof was starting to sag. The sign hadn't been changed or taken down—it still said 98.9 cents a gallon.

Those days are long gone, he thought to himself. The department had made a special line item in the budget last year just for gasoline. It used to be included with the costs for vehicle maintenance—it was now more than the maintenance budget.

Around ten o'clock he saw a lone man weaving slightly and heading down the street. He didn't look quite right. The man's bent head turned from side to side. Although walking slowly he seemed to be unusually alert. The weaving man fit the description Lupe had given him.

There were two younger women across the street. The drunk seemed to be watching them out of the corner of his eye. As Tom approached, he could see the man's hair sticking out of the old ball cap's adjusting strap, dark brown; he knew for sure that it was the perp Lupe had described.

Tom walked swiftly towards the man and warily drew his pistol.

"Stop! Police officer. Put your hands on your head!"

The man did as he was told. Delano read him his Miranda. He put his badge and ID away with his left hand and then handcuffed the man. Tom took one more good look to make sure. The perp looked just as Lupe had described. He loaded him into the vehicle and he and Mike took him to the police station.

The first interrogator read the man his rights once more as they seated him in a hard wooden chair. The detective had turned a tape recorder on. After two hours of questioning, the man finally started talking—he was getting weary and broke down.

Tom thought of Lupe. He wished he could tell her he had caught this guy. The man's right wrist was still purple and he had a bruise under one eye.

That girl is something else, Tom said to himself, *I would never want her to get mad at me. I wonder how Lupe is doing back in New York?*

Lupe watched the street for over an hour. Finally she did see a patrol car, *they really are watching out for me.*

Ten days later Lupe couldn't take it any longer. She kept imagining one of Ladero's men breaking in the door during the night. She felt confined—like she was in a prison.

She slipped out the back of the building just as the patrol car rounded the corner and headed in the other direction. She walked towards the subway but instead; she hailed a taxi to Brooklyn. She gave the driver a fifty-cent tip and apologized, he nodded that he understood. Once near, she got out and walked to the Greyhound bus station on Livingston, a roundabout way, but she didn't want to take a chance that Scippio's men might spot her. She figured they would be watching the subway, the bus, and train stations near where she had worked the hotels.

Forty-five minutes later she was on a bus heading for Columbus. She would buy a new ticket to Dayton when she got there. She was running òut of money and she didn't want to leave a trail, but there was not much choice, *I will just have to risk it.*

Lupe didn't feel safe until the bus had passed through the Lincoln Tunnel and they were on the turnpike. She slept until Allentown. The bus popped onto the Harrisburg Turnpike and they had a rest stop at Bedford.

A new driver took over. They stopped for a few minutes at Wheeling and then on to Columbus. Her ticket took her to there, *I will worry about getting further west then.*

CHAPTER TWELVE

Carlos Cados opened the double doors to the small banquet room in the La Paloma, *how many times have I done this?* It was rhetorical. He didn't answer himself.

In a few moments men started filing into the room. Carlos kept track. As soon as all nineteen where there, he closed and locked the doors.

"Señores! We are discussing our next operation. We were at first blamed for the explosion that was part of a Muslim Jihad. We will take credit for the one we are planning within a few hours just after it happens. We don't take credit for others."

There were a few nods, they all agreed.

"We are not immune to harm done by others; we are often blamed. We Basques want the foreign Spanish government to leave us alone and our brothers on the other side of the Pyrenees Mountains want the same of France."

"We will need five of you to acquire enough explosives to sink an old ship in a harbor. The harbor has not been picked yet," he really had picked the harbor and the ship, he just wasn't ready to divulge its location yet.

"The last elections in Spain were not good for us. We will pick an old ship and one with no people on board. We just want to make a lot of noise and send a message."

"The message is: That we are **still here**!" Carlos emphasized "...still here..!" He pounded his fist on the tabletop.

Immediately five young hands shot up. Carlos remembered when he was young, how excited he had been for the cause—to make a mark.

The Basques had been in torment for over four hundred years. The Spanish Civil War and World War Two had been their only respite.

Carlos was over 65 and he was slowing down, in fact his next birthday was soon; this last fall. He could tell the slowness; sometimes he wished that he could just go away—maybe to America. It was time to retire. Let the younger men he had trained do the work. The Spanish government thought he was dead anyway. He and Mikel had arranged for his death a few years ago. There were stones buried in a grave with his name carved on the cheap headstone above. There was somebody's body in the casket.

The twenty men planned and schemed for two more hours. Just as the meeting was breaking up, there was a hard knock on the door. Carlos opened the door a crack; it was only the part time gardener from the Church. He mowed the lawns and sometimes weeded the flower beds. Carlos let him in.

"Señor Carlos. There has been someone asking questions about your family."

"Who has been asking, Juan?"

"I do not know. Someone though. The Padre is excited. A letter came from America. It was asking about the Hirschmann family and the Cados family."

"Si. That is my real name—Hirschmann. I will go see the Padre."

Carlos opened the doors wide and the men started filtering out into the hallway. They went in several directions. Two men wandered off to the hotel bar.

Carlos had known Juan for twenty-five years, *a good and honest man, he is Basque. I hope someone is not stirring up trouble for me. If the police start looking...Carlos* started down the winding, cobblestone path towards the street, his light blond and graying hair; blowing in the light breeze. He sometimes worried about "his" grave filled with a strange body. If the police found it...what would they know?

He buttoned the top button of his collar and straightened his tie. Carlos was going to Church.

CHAPTER THIRTEEN

It was damp out and the sun had been gone for hours. Lupe put on her headscarf and walked to the Columbus ticket window. She asked the price of a ticket to Dayton. The young, part-time agent told her the price.

"I cannot afford that much. How close can you get me?" She shoved her remaining money across to him over the worn counter.

He saw her ticket stub from Brooklyn and noticed her clean, but well-worn clothes. There was a patch, a neat patch, in the left sleeve.

He felt sorry for her, "If I sold you a ticket all the way to Dayton for less than full price, I would be in a lot of trouble, but they don't pay any attention to the ones I hand write. I can get you to Springfield. You'll have to tell the driver to stop, as we don't have a regular stop there. He can let you off near an off-ramp. It will be late at night an no traffic. Is that OK? That's the best I can do."

"I'll take it," she didn't have a clue where Springfield was, but figured it would get her closer to Dayton.

"Fine. You have four dollars change." He had just rounded off her money and gave her back the bills. She was fifteen dollars short. Lupe never caught on. The agent had a big heart. Besides, this time of night, the bus had sixteen empty seats. He had some freedom to override certain charges on hand written tickets when the bus was not full. He remembered when he had tried hitchhiking during the Gulf War. He usually ended up buying a bus ticket.

Lupe walked out to the bus and gave the driver her ticket, "Please let me off at Springfield."

"No problem young lady. We don't go into Springfield. I'll just tell my relief driver and he'll pull off the highway and right back on again. I only drive six hours with a thirty-minute break in between—this is my break now. I have a little more than two hours to drive."

He turned towards the passengers standing by the double doors, "Take your seat please. Just pick one, there's plenty of empties."

It had been a long twelve hours. It seemed like both busses had stopped at every possible stop. Eight miles after letting Lupe off near the Springfield off ramp; the bus came to a stop. There had been an accident and the officers were letting one vehicle go through at a time.

The new driver promptly forgot the young girl who had gotten off at the Springfield turnoff. He had intended to mention it to his Supervisor. Something had seemed odd. He grumbled to himself, *this accident will make me late. My wife will already be fixing breakfast.*

He yapped silently at the highway patrol, with their 'flying wheel' patches on their jackets and the "idiots" that had caused the wreck, *blockheads—never around when you need them.*

Four days later, when the driver was handed an all points bulletin flyer by the division boss; it meant nothing to him.

Springfield wasn't a very big town and Lupe decided she didn't want to explore. She walked against the light to the far side, through the underpass for local traffic, and stuck out her thumb. She would hitchhike to Dayton. She stood by a sign that said:

DAYTON

37 MILES

She held her hand on it to indicate she was going there. The first car to stop was an older lady in a small van.

"Get in please. I can't stay awake and I need you to talk to me. My youngest daughter is in the hospital having a baby and I'm late. I have never picked up a hitchhiker, but you look okay."

Lupe did her bidding; she talked incessantly the next few miles. The lady stayed awake.

"I am taking Rip Rap Road for a ways and then cutting over. I'm going directly to the hospital and after I see my daughter I will find you a ride, somehow, to the center of Dayton."

"Thank you. I'm not familiar with Dayton."

Lupe went inside the hospital with her. She looked around, this is a large place.

There was dust in the corners and the windows needed washing. The door brass in the lobby was dull—not at all like the polished hotel brass back in New York. The place needed some work. She had an idea.

She looked for the administrative office. Lupe soon found the office and next to the door was:

HUMAN RESOURCES

Under the larger sign was a black and white plastic nameplate: James L. Warner, Dir.

On a small table were some applications. She filled one out and wrote down a fake address on Harshman Avenue. She wrote 'no phone' in the block for a phone number. The top of the form asked for a name. Lupe used Sally Lindstrum again.

She gave references in Columbus that she made up. Lupe had unconsciously remembered some of the streets as they had zoomed by on the highway.

The office clerk was just coming to work. She noticed Lupe sitting outside as she slipped off her light jacket and hung it on a hanger, "May I help you?"

"Sss…yes. I am looking for work. Anything. Cleaning perhaps."

"Sure. Have a seat. Mr. Warner will be here shortly. I am sure we have openings. We almost always do. Nobody stays long in the janitorial department. I have a list here somewhere," she rummaged around on her desk.

"Oh! Yes! We are indeed looking for a cleaning person. We need two actually."

Charlene busied herself with opening cabinets and unlocking the inner office double doors. She reached in and turned on the lights in Mr. Warner's office. "I'm Charlene Moore by-the-way. If you need something, just holler."

A few minutes later a pleasant looking man around fifty-five years old came in. Charlene said good morning and handed him Lupe's application. He nodded and looked her way.

Lupe sat for ten minutes more. A low male voice asked Charlene to send her in.

She was hired at three dollars above minimum wage and she was to start right away. The hospital cleaning crew had been short-handed for a month. In ninety days, the probationary period, she would get a raise to nine dollars, a seventy-five cent raise. And her benefits would start then.

Charlene said, "Here. Take this paper to Sam Brady. He is the head of maintenance and he contracts or hires all of the janitorial services and people. Room B-110. That's in the basement where the X-Ray and CT scan rooms are," she pointed, "take the elevator to the right. His office is by the heating and cooling system and UPS emergency power equipment at the far end. You can't miss his office; he has an American flag tacked over his door. And a picture of Madam Nu's daughter in uniform."

Lupe wasn't sure who Madam Nu was, but it must be some important person attached to the hospital.

Lupe was only lost once—she had to ask directions. The basement was larger than she thought. It had three main aisles and four cross-aisles. A set of concrete stairs led down to another level. It had a warning sign:

FUEL—DANGER

The steel fireproof door was locked. She supposed she would need to learn the entire hospital and offices.

She memorized things as she walked down the hallway—X-ray rooms, special examining rooms, MRI, pharmacy storage, employee cafeteria, and the locations of the two sets of elevators; one elevator was deep; for gurneys she supposed. She didn't go to the other side and look at the elevators there—she guessed there would be two more placed just like these only opposite.

She noticed by looking at the maps posted, that all of the patient beds were on the above three floors. She would memorize them later. She finally saw the UPS room. It had **Universal Power Supply** in small letters, stamped on an equipment rack inside. The door was partly open. An odd buzzing noise came from the room.

She could see a huge, but silent, John Deere engine in the far corner, *that must be what the fuel room is for.*

She spotted the office, the American flag needed cleaning. And Madam Nu's daughter was pretty. She read the caption. It dawned on her this was from the Vietnam War.

She looked at the flag closer; it looked like smoke instead of dirt. And there were two holes near one corner. She could run her finger through them if she tried. The holes were dirty.

She got it, *this flag was probably flying over a US compound and was shot at by an enemy. There were some odd words underneath:* **Thợ máy** — she found out later they meant "Electrician."

Sam Brady seemed nice. He asked her to have a chair. He had read her application. Charlene had sent it down by FAX a few minutes before. She handed him the paper Charlene had given her.

"I grew up in Columbus. I never heard of Morton Street. Where is it?"

Lupe stumbled, " I ah….it's in a new subdivision on the east edge of town—almost in the country."

Sam smiled. He figured it out, "I know the feeling. You're out of work huh? I couldn't get a job for six months back in the World when I came home from Nam. And you are not from hereabouts. You sound like east coast. I won't say a word as long as you are a willing worker."

"Oh! Jes, I will work hard," she slipped into her accent; she was nervous.

"I can start you right now if you want," he looked at his watch, "what time did you get here?"

"I was waiting by the office door a few minutes before it opened. It must have been just before 8:15."

"OK. Stay until quitting time and we'll call it a full day. Here are the hours and we don't punch a clock anymore. We used to." He handed here a schedule slip, "Take a normal forty-five minute lunch."

That first day was a day of confusion. The main part of the hospital was easy. It was the wings that had been added at different times that caused the confusion. She couldn't fathom the numerical sequence of the rooms—they seemed out of order.

The second floor was not so confusing. The floor plan didn't include some of the wings and the second story part of the building was divided into A, B, and C. And all of the patient room numbers started with A2-1, B2-1, or C2-1. The third floor was numbered in a similar manner. That numbering was easy.

Sam saw her dilemma for the first floor and the basement and finally drew a sketch of all floors so that she could put them in the pocket of her new, pale-green uniform. There were **YOU ARE HERE** maps on the walls, but they were old and out of date.

Late that afternoon she walked from the hospital towards the Miami River. One of the nurses had given her directions and told her not to go as far as Mad Creek. She walked almost two miles before the neighborhood looked like something she could afford.

Across the road that followed the river, there was a billboard advertising the "Dayton Dragons" who were located on Fifth Third Field, what a strange address, she thought. The silly looking dragon was holding a baseball bat.

She turned and walked another half mile west before she found something that she might be able to afford. Lupe spotted an older building. It was clean, but seemed out of place amongst the imposing condos and townhouses scattered up and down the street on both sides. She knew about where she was. Lupe had found Keenan Street on the map back at the hospital and she had crossed it over ten minutes ago.

She went inside. There was a middle-aged lady at the desk; "I am looking for a small room that I can cook in. I just went to work at the hospital and I won't have a check until Friday."

"Honey, you won't get a check until next week on Friday. They hold back a week. I know all about that hospital. I used to work there in the janitorial department."

"That's where I work. I'm in trouble. I have no place to stay. I only have three dollars and some change."

The older lady looked at Lupe. Almost like she was looking at herself through the hospital's X-ray, "I'll tell you what. Let me see your badge."

Lupe showed it to her. It was temporary, but it had the hospital logo on it.

"OK. I'll let you have the room on trust. I have three empties and no takers anyway. I'll let you have the smallest and in the back. No view and only one window. It's really small."

"Oh! Thank you. Thank you. I'll take it and I will pay you the next week when I get paid."

"Fill this form out and sign this slip." Lupe did.

"Here's yo'als keys, that small one is the postal mail box key. It's out front. Your box is 5–A, the same as the room number. By the way, make yourself a lunch each day from my refrigerator until you get paid. There is bread, lunchmeat, lettuce, and all kinds of stuff. And colas. I'm by myself and some of it will go bad anyway. It's over there." The black lady pointed to the left-hand corner.

Lupe picked up the old Army duffle bag and headed to her new room. It had a tiny refrigerator, no freezer, and there was a two-burner stove sitting on four cast iron legs on the counter. A long flexible hose went through a hole in the counter top and connected to a gas outlet under the single sink.

The room was more than twice the size of her attic room back in New York and she had lived there for more than a year, *this is Paradise!*

CHAPTER FOURTEEN

Lieutenant Jimmy Fagan knocked on Ileana Montero's door. He usually stayed in the office and only worked big cases. This one interested him and he wasn't sure why. Ileana carefully answered the door; she kept the slide chain attached.

"*Si.* Yes."

"I am here to talk to Miss Lupe Guzman. Would you ask her to come to the door please," he showed her his badge and ID card.

"She is no here. She has gone again and no letter this time and no marks in the phone book. I do not know where she is."

"Damn!" Jimmy said under his breath as he walked away. He drove slowly back to the station, *would she go back to Ohio? She believed in the Fates so it says in the report. Hmmm, maybe so.*

When he was back in his office, he picked up the phone and punched an outside line. He had Tom Delano's name written on his desk pad and Dayton was underlined.

Jimmy got a busy signal, *I'll put out a bulletin again.*

He punched up the old one on the computer and changed the date. Jimmy also changed the hair color from blond to light brown. He had remembered her hair and the ink-darkened hair on Tom Delano's flysheet photo.

CHAPTER FIFTEEN

Carlos spotted the Padre in the churchyard near the cemetery. He was trimming rose bushes. "Padre!"

"Ah! Good to see you. I have missed you on Sunday."

"You know me Padre, I come when I can. The money comes for the children, Si?"

"Ah *Si. Muchas gracias.*"

"Someone is looking for my father?"

"I think so. Maybe they look for you as well," the Padre was Basque and knew of the "death" of Carlos.

"Who?"

"Someone from America," the Padre handed Carlos the letter.

"I do not know of this person. I wonder why she inquires?"

Carlos copied down the address in a little notebook that he always carried. He looked out of the garden towards the street. A Guardia Civil patrol car cruised by. They were looking the other way—not interested in the Churchyard.

"Gracias Padre. I will see why this person is looking for the Cados familia. Please, keep the letter. I kept the American stamps. My nephew collects them."

Carlos hurried back to his car, *I will tell Mikel Andraka tonight. He has been to America. He will know more.*

Carlos and Mikel had been a part of the Basque ETA* for many years. They had never been caught since they started working together. They prided themselves in never blowing up anything with people around—whatever it was they exploded; no one had ever been killed in the many years they had been doing this.

*Euskadi Ta Askatasun; Basque Country and Liberty.

Carlos called Mikel on his cell phone. No answer. He turned right and drove towards his leased home instead. He had lived here almost four years under another name.

Time to move again, he thought—in fact it is past time. He always drove around the block first—sometimes he circled

53

twice. There was nobody behind him. He backed in under some trees. There was no garage. He liked his van facing the street.

He opened the cellar door at the side of the house and walked down the hand-formed, clay steps. There was a locked steel door at the bottom. He entered. At the third row of wine racks, in the back, there was a hidden switch. He flipped it. A small door opened. He stooped and went inside. He and Mikel had installed this themselves. It had taken almost four months to complete; they were only able to work on it part time.

He looked about the room. It had not been used for a while. The last time, Carlos had hidden a French Basque, Bastien Jacques inside. This hidden room was complete with a cot, closet, toilet, kerosene lamp, and a table with two chairs.

A small box was under the table. Carlos opened it with a hidden key. There were some old yellowed papers inside. The two on top were in Spanish. The dried out, rubber band broke. Carlos looked hastily through the pile of papers. There were only these top two in Spanish, the rest were in German.

HIRSCHMANN was written on the top line of the paper in the second pile. Carlos had decided long ago that this was his real family name. The letter that the Padre had gave Ileana Hirschmann's nee name along with Montero at the bottom. Carlos had not looked in this old box for over a decade and he had forgotten her married name. He knew who she was.

Carlos brushed his gray-blond hair out of his blue eyes, *maybe I will go to America. I am getting too old for all of this*. He was tired of trying to weaken the foreign Spanish. They seemed to only grow stronger.

Carlos often wondered if the Basque people on both sides of the border would ever have their own country again. Carlos had read much about the Basque. They were here first. A very ancient people—leftover Cro-Magnons some scholars said.

The book he had read, said they were here in Spain ten thousand years before the first ancestors of the Spanish arrived; the Visigoths, Kelts, and much later, Romans. Perhaps even twenty thousand years ago. Certainly way before the last Ice Age.

Maybe the Basque ate dinosaurio for dinner. No, wrong millennium. Perhaps the grande y muy peludo elefante. Ah. Si. The hairy mammoth. He laughed at himself.

At least the ETA had some success in the 1970s. Franco had loosened his hold somewhat just before he died. King Juan Carlos had let some of the Basque people out of jail after 1975.

Mikel Andraka had been one of them and Carlos had trained Mikel. He had met him on one of his trips to Vitoria. The young man was willing and ready. He had already participated in one of the semi-violent, college street riots and that was why he had received only an eighteen-month sentence to prison. Not so much violence on the part of the Basque students, but of the Spanish police. Mikel had served less than a year. They let him out in 1999. After all these years, the former college student was still bitter.

Carlos decided he would see what paperwork he would need to enter the United States. His cell phone rang. It was Mikel. "*Si.*" He listened, "I will be right there."

Carlos pulled carefully out of the small gravel driveway to the left and swung a U-turn. He needed to go north. Mikel was sipping a heavy red wine when Carlos arrived. He had ordered one for Carlos. They talked for thirty minutes about normal things.

"Carlos. I have an idea. I have been to New York City three times. I have relatives and friends there. I will go for you and find out why this person seeks you. If the Spanish find out, you are in much trouble my amigo."

"I will think on it," he paused and drank the rest of his wine, "Perhaps that is a good idea. You go and find why this person is writing and seeking the Cados family, I am supposed to be dead."

Carlos thought he knew, *do I want to find my sister?*

He wasn't sure. *I don't remember her. Perhaps a vague shadow or is that my imagination—must be. I was only a baby a few months old, or was I older.*

He actually didn't know when they had been separated.

Mikel was an amigo—a true friend.

Mikel drained his wine glass and left hurriedly. He had paperwork to fill out.

"Adios Mikel." The door swung shut.

Carlos drove slowly back to his house—thinking. He backed in under the tree as he always did after circling the block twice. He slipped into the house through the back door and made sure all of the blackout curtains were pulled. He never turned on a light unless they were.

After years of self-training, Carlos slept with one eye open, or so it seemed. He would get up several times a night and look through the curtains about the house. After forty years he was permanently a light sleeper. If a dog barked somewhere, he was wide-awake with a gun in his hand.

Tonight was no different, as tired as he was; he got up four times and peered outside. Each time the night was quiet.

CHAPTER SIXTEEN

Lupe liked the work in the hospital and she liked the people she had met. The head nurse, Linda McMorris, was exceptionally nice. Lupe cleaned some things that had not been cleaned in a long time. She came in a little early and left a little late. "Sally" was noticed and remarked about. Lupe's grandmother always told her to "....give the boss one-hundred and one percent no matter what they pay you...." Lupe remembered.

Tom Delano looked at the computer screen. There was a bulletin out again to look for Lupe Guzman.

She has done it again, Tom said to himself. The New York Police figured she had run again to Ohio. Tom looked through the database arrest sheets back about ten days in the surrounding three counties. He sorted through the females and looked at the descriptions. Nothing in the database matched Lupe.

Surely she wouldn't come back to Dayton.

He wondered though. *Had our connection been strong enough?* He opened his wallet. He had found her photo in JPEG on the police net and printed out a copy on glossy paper, *indeed she is pretty.* He liked her smile too.

Tom remembered the train ride. The smell of her hair had stimulated both his nostrils and his thoughts. He found that he really liked her. Tom came out of his daze, *maybe she is indeed back in Dayton.*

It was his turn to drive, "Sarge, let's take a look down by Findley. They are looking for Lupe Guzman again. She split." Tom drove in ever closing circles for the next forty-five minutes. Nothing!

Tom drove in that general area off and on over the next two weeks. One day, "I think we ought to drive across the river. We haven't been up there for a while."

"That's not our beat."

"I'll call in and say we are going to lunch."

"Go ahead. I gotta sandwich. I don't know what you are going to eat."

"I'll grab a cup of coffee and a doughnut. That's all we cops ever eat anyway—right?"

"Yeah!" They both laughed.

Lupe had just finished her work cleaning the emergency hallway when she heard sirens. The van pulled up and one of the crew jumped in. They were short one person.

One of the medics, George Keller, yelled "Hey you! Sally! Hop in! You can help carry our equipment. The call says this is a big one. Put on this jacket. It belongs to Sandy. She's out sick today."

Lupe dropped her cleaning rag and climbed in behind George. They sped off to the southeast towards the main highway—sirens squealing. She thought, *this is exciting.*

An SUV was on its side and a motorcycle was crunched against a divider. The rider was across the concrete, lying in the grass. George and the other medic grabbed their equipment and ran to the SUV. There were people inside.

Lupe went to the biker. Blood was gushing from his neck. Lupe squeezed the gash with two fingers and pressed on a large vein with her thumb—it was a long stretch and not easy to do, but she had long fingers. The fellow was moaning. She used her left hand and pushed his helmet off. The man was not very old, perhaps twenty-five.

She held on tight. The blood stopped. He continued to moan. Saliva was coming from his lips, he gave a choking sound; Lupe stuck her left index finger into his mouth and gently forced his teeth apart. The young man started breathing through his partly open mouth. The saliva was pink. He went unconscious.

She yelled, "George! Come quickly! I think this one's hurt inside."

George ran over, "Yes. Something punctured his chest. The handle-bar maybe or the throttle handle."

He pulled the leather jacket back and ripped open the shirt. Pinkish blood was coming out and foam. The biker's lung was indeed punctured. George pulled a plastic, adhesive sheet from the bandage bag and sealed the hole in the young man's chest.

Lupe held onto the gash in his neck.

"Sally, I'll take over and seal off the neck wound. Please go help Bill. He has his hands full. There is a little kid in the back. She's crying and saying something—just a baby learning to talk. Here's some alcohol, douse your hands."

Tom Delano was two miles away, he punched two buttons on the patrol car's radio, a dispatcher was directing a couple of cars to the scene of an accident.

Mike Strand looked up, "We'll go through the warehouse district and then on over there. The accident will be gone long before we can get out of this traffic."

"We could turn on the lights and siren."

"Wouldn't help much. Where is everyone ahead of us going to go? It is packed with cars. Bad time of day."

They forced their way off the highway by turning onto the dirt and grass. In a few minutes they cruised the warehouse area— nothing interesting—this was a pretend run anyway.

They found the highway again and followed a surface road. When they finally arrived, one of the wrecker drivers was sweeping up glass. The last patrol car was pulling away. The emergency van was long gone.

Lupe was dressed in her best blouse. The hospital Administrator had set up an appointment to talk with her at 9:00 o'clock. It was 8:50. Lupe liked to be early. She had streaked her hair. Her blond roots were starting to show.

She only sat there for a couple of minutes.

"Come in Sally! Come in! I have heard more good things about you. How would you like to take some training courses and work with the 911 crews?"

She was startled for just a second, and then said, "I would like that Mr. Slade."

"How did you learn to stop arteries from bleeding and how to take care of accident victims? Do you have a background in emergency measures? Have you had CPR?"

Lupe was quiet for a moment. How could she explain? She had seen countless knife wounds in New York and many auto accidents. She had watched paramedics "doctor" people on the sidewalks right in front of where she worked—schlepping hotel client's bags and suitcases. She had watched them many times. Always curious.

She smiled up at Mr. Slade, "I watch a lot of TV."

Frank Slade smiled as well, "I don't think so, but we'll not discuss it. You will start class right here in the hospital on Monday. One of the medics you assisted is teaching the first class. Please show up at 7:00."

He raised from his leather chair and turned, "Is that OK? What time do you come to work now?"

"I'm here at six."

"Wonderful! And stop by from time to time. I would like to know how you like the class. This is our first time. Usually we hire someone from outside that has had a year or so of medical college. The beginning med students need the money. The hospital board, and me, decided we would start teaching and promoting from within." He smiled again.

Lupe took a short breath. Didn't he know she had not finished high school? She rose and turned towards the door, "Thank you Sss...Mr. Slade." She knew he had seen her application. Maybe it didn't matter.

There were six students in the class on Monday. She was the only female. She recognized two of the younger men as orderlies, they already worked in the emergency and trauma wing.

The first thirty minutes each student told a little bit about themselves. Lupe made up her life story. And then the instructor, George Keller, spent a few minutes talking about himself. He had been at this hospital for twelve years and had worked his way up to supervisor over the emergency response 911 unit.

He had gone to the local two-year college at night and had gone to Chicago for seminars on fast action emergency unit response. George had also flown to New York City a few times and attended three lengthy seminars on the emergency 9/11 responses after the airplanes crashed the two towers and the Pentagon—learning about both the good and the bad.

George Keller was married and had two sons. Both in soccer, it kept him and his wife busy when not working. His wife, Martha, had been his childhood sweetheart. His grandparents had left Germany just after the First World War and he could speak decent German. Lupe liked his hearty outlook and his openness.

She felt badly; she had made up the entire story about herself.

He rolled down a large anatomy chart in full color. Lupe could see veins, muscles, and internal cutaways of organs.

"You will be expected to learn around 90% of what you see on this chart. I have some small ones printed out. When you leave this morning, take one with you. On the backside of the cardboard are the answers. You just cut it out with scissors and overlay it on the chart. The arrows pointing to the anatomy parts line up with the Latin names on the overlay. Study it. Pull the overlay off and self-test yourself as many times as it takes. There will be a real test in two weeks."

"Now I have a slide show for the class. Sam pull those blinds please. Sally would you please close the forward blinds."

'Sally Lindstrum' rose, moved to the wall, pulled the cord, and twisted the long plastic rod.

The slide show started. It was about driving safely in a high speed, heavy vehicle; with lights and sirens blaring. Lupe didn't make much sense out of it. She had never driven a car—it looked very dangerous.

CHAPTER SEVENTEEN

Twelve days after the meeting with Carlos, he was in New York and landing at JFK. Mikel Andraka showed his passport and visitor permit at the customs gate. He had only a small carry-on bag. The US Customs agent ran a wand over him and waved him on after looking inside the bag. There was nothing in the computer concerning him.

He caught a taxi, "Take me for please to Spanish Harlem—Edlons. It is a store on......"

"Yeah! Yeah! I know where Edlons is," he shoved the taxi in drive and took off down a side street leaving JFK quickly behind. It was the end of his midnight to morning shift and he was tired. He was in no mood to talk to foreigners.

Morning traffic wasn't bad. Forty-five minutes later the taxi pulled up near the curb in front of Edlons. Mikel handed the driver some money, "Change you keep for the onura—how you say—a favor!"

"Tip! The word is tip." The driver shook his head and mumbled something about, 'damned foreigners.'

As Mikel stepped up on the curb, he was immediately jostled by the sidewalk crowd going to work, and said to himself, "Maybe this place deserves no favor." Only he said it in Basque, onura. He made his way through the store's revolving doors. Once inside he asked for Señor Plano Aniel.

A uniformed guard responded, "He is on the third floor. There are company offices there. You are not allowed on that floor unless you have business." After 9/11, many of the stores had tightened security.

"Please announce to him. He will talk with me."

The guard was reluctant, but he called the security desk on the third floor. There was a pause, the voice on the other end said, "Mr. Aniel wants you to repeat the name." He did.

"OK! Send him up on elevator three," the voice spoke over the small speakerphone. Mikel recognized his friend Plano's voice.

Mikel walked into the office, "Hola! We need to smoke some kasto like the old days at the university."

"No my hermano. Not anymore. I don't smoke that stuff. I even stopped smoking—period!"

They embraced. "It has been a long time. What—eleven years?"

"I think so," they both started talking in Basque.

Thirty minutes later Mikel had a gun, converted money, and an address where he could stay. He walked out on the street and flagged down a cab. In twenty-five minutes he was in Spanish Harlem and walking up to the third floor of the old tenement building.

He had seen Ileana's name on the mailbox tag as he walked along the downstairs hallway. He knocked. Ileana Montero answered the door quizzically, the door chain in place, "Yes."

"I am looking for Ileana Montero," he spoke in Spanish.

She thought his mode of speech and quaint accent were odd, "I am Ileana. Why do you ask?"

"I have come from Spain. You have written a letter to our Padre. I was sent to inquire further. I am only a bystander."

She was astounded, "Please come in and have a seat, I wrote asking of my younger brother. He was separated from me when I was young. Do you know of him?"

"Perhaps I do," he held up the letter she had mailed. The Padre had given it to him minus the corner where the stamp was, "in this letter you were seeking members of the Cados family. How do you know of this family?"

"From an office in Madrid. I wrote a letter and they answered."

"It was that easy."

Mikel was now concerned, *was his compadre safe? Had she opened up something? Would the government start looking for Carlos. He had been listed as dead for over seven years now.*

"No! Not really. It took me many letters and many years to find this much. Thirty-five years to be exact."

Ileana walked to the sink. She had prepared coffee for breakfast earlier, "Would you like some coffee? It is over an hour old."

The window smashed! Ileana fell back against the old refrigerator and slumped forward towards the floor. She almost dropped the pot—she slid it on the counter in the last seconds.

Mikel jumped straight to the window—there was a movement across the way in another tenement building. In the open window of the other building he saw a dark man with a scar on his cheek, dismantling a rifle. Mikel turned quickly and rushed through the apartment door.

Mikel ran for the stairs and took them two at a time. He was on the street and around the corner in less than three minutes. He darted across the street, dodging traffic. A dark car was just speeding away towards the river. It looked almost new. There was no license plate. He saw a booster cell phone antenna on the right; the antenna was bent at an angle.

Mikel went back upstairs. Ileana was sitting in a chair with a towel wrapped around her shoulder. It was red—streaked with blood.

"I will call the *Guardia Civil*."

"You mean the police. We say police here."

"I will call them," he picked up the phone.

"The phone is no working. I cannot afford it anymore. They keep raising the price. I could get a special rate, but I won't do that," she had a proud tilt to her chin as she spoke.

Mikel headed for the street again. Just as he opened the door, one of two policemen, was reaching for the doorknob.

"My friend Ileana has been shot. Come with me please. Quickly!"

They examined Ileana. 911 had already called for paramedics, and the sirens could be heard in the distance. Someone in the building had heard the shot, ran to Ileana's door, saw her, and called. The young man was still standing by the stairway.

One policeman looked at the shattered window and then looked straight across into the old tenement window. It was easy to see what had happened. The medics arrived.

"We'll get a statement from her at the hospital. We'll follow the van."

As they walked down the stairs, Mikel Andraka told them most of what he saw and described the man. He didn't tell them that he thought he could find the car. He signed a paper. They left and Mikel started walking up the street towards the river. He checked on Ileana every day.

Two days later he walked south. He spotted a similar parked car over thirty blocks away; then he saw the bent cell phone antenna, it was the right car. No license plate. Mikel waited in the shadows by the alley mouth. Twenty minutes later he recognized the scar faced man who had dismantled the rifle. He was unlocking the car.

Mikel slipped up behind him and pressed the gun into his back, "Unlock the behind door. Slide under the steering. Be much careful. I will be in back pointing this to you." He thrust the gun hard into the man's back.

"Si. Ho Kay."

Mikel started speaking in Spanish, "Now. Drive slowly and make a right at the next corner."

"Stop here. Why did you shoot my new friend?"

"It was an accident."

"How do you mean?"

"We thought it was another *rubia* named Lupe, a young one. This *persona* was nothing but an old lady."

"In Spain you would pay for that accident with your life. America is more liberal than Spain," he shot Garcia in the shoulder in almost the same spot as Ileana. He hurriedly left the car. He had touched nothing. Mikel knew of America's passion for fingerprints. He had watched old Black and White movies with Bogart. In one movie Bogart had his fingerprints removed by an old doctor.

Garcia had passed out in the front seat. His moaning was heard an hour later and a police car pulled up and stopped. They had been called. The dismantled rifle was still in the trunk.

"Too bad Ladero was not riding with Garcia," one of the policemen thought to himself.

Mikel rode a bus to the intersection near his hotel. He would wait a few days and visit Ileana once again. He knew that eventually he would find all of the shooter's compadres. He had not seen them, but he knew there were more than just the one. There had to be a *hefe*, a boss.

CHAPTER EIGHTEEN

Lupe stood by the classroom door. She had scored 96% on the anatomy quiz. She was pleased and the instructor was pleased. She discovered that a lot of the Latin names for body parts were similar to Spanish.

Mr. Warner heard about the test that afternoon. He told Frank Slade. Mr. Slade found her cleaning the brass on the main front doors.

"Miss Lindstrum. Would you come with me please?"

She set her bucket and sponge aside and followed him down the hallway; to herself, *I have not done anything, I don't think.*

"I am taking you out of the facilities and maintenance department completely. You will be transferred to the emergency response unit as a helper at first. As you finish more class work, we will give you more and more to do. Is that something you would like?"

"Oh yes. That is wonderful. I want to help and be useful. Thank you Mr. Slade."

"Fine. Turn in all of your equipment and go to the Head Nurse and see about getting a different badge. I have already notified them," he rose and reached out his hand, she shook his hand and thanked him again.

He said, "This time you get your picture taken." He smiled. "Oh! There will be a raise of course."

Lupe walked out into the hall and almost jumped in the air. She said aloud, "How am I so lucky? God has been watching over me and so have the Fates." She almost whistled she was so happy. It was just about lunchtime, *I will go tell my landlord.*

She and the landlord, Aunt Bessie, as she liked to be called, had become best of friends. Lupe had finally confided in her and told her that she was Lupe Guzman. Aunt Bessie had agreed that she had done the best thing. She might be dead had she stayed in New York City.

Lupe was so excited that she jogged to her apartment building. Aunt Bessie was in the front office watching a game show re-run. She saw Lupe running up the sidewalk and clicked MUTE.

"I have a new job. I am so excited. I will be working with the 911 ambulance emergency crews and the paramedics."

"That's wonderful. I knew you could do it," she rose and hugged Lupe. She had helped her study—reading the Latin names and Lupe would point to them on the chart.

"All of that studying did you good. When are you going to tell them who you really are? It was OK when you were just a janitor, now that you have a more important job at the hospital, you must say something. You cannot keep quiet. You are part if a team."

"I want to tell Mr. Warner, but I know the Ladero gang is still looking for me. I can identify all three of them. I'm afraid to go back to New York City and I'm afraid to go to the police here."

"Well you have been here all this time and nobody has come around. How would they know that you came back to Ohio?'

"I don't know, but they know things. I should contact my grandmother somehow. I could write a letter, but I don't trust the mailman that comes to my grandmother's. He grew up there and knows all of Ladero's men."

"I would not wait too long. It is not fair to your crew and Mr. Warner. I have known Jim Warner for twenty years. He'll understand if you level with him. And it is not fair to your grandmother."

"*Si.* You are right. I will wait a week, and ask for a meeting with him. Swear for him to quiet be," she slipped back into her dialect, "I must tell Sr. Slade as well." She sat quietly for a few moments, unconsciously glancing at the silent game show on TV. Her foot was wiggling.

"I cannot be still, Aunt Bessie. Let's walk to the little neighborhood café and I will buy you lunch. I have thirty minutes yet and the café is over half way back to the hospital."

Bessie locked the door, hung the paper clock on the door, moved the hands to 1:00 o'clock, and the two women walked quickly to the north.

After lunch Lupe was given her new badge. It said:

EMERGENCY TECHNICIAN

She snapped it on her pocket and smiled. She headed towards the emergency entrance hallway.

CHAPTER NINETEEN

It was Thursday. Tom and his partner were driving towards the hospital. The Sergeant had been asked to speak and give a presentation to a new class of emergency response students. Tom was going to run the overhead projector from the station's laptop. They had a digitized slide show.

Tom set up the equipment and was busy plugging in the final cords. The students filed in. Lupe didn't notice Tom. He was behind the table on his knees plugging in cables.

The students sat down. The Sergeant introduced himself. It was too late. Officer Tom Delano stood up and was looking right at Lupe. Lupe was now almost blond again. For just a second he thought he had made a mistake. Lupe held her index finger to her lips.

Tom sat back down and shook his head towards the door. Lupe knew what he meant. She nodded. Tom clicked the first frame.

At the first break, Tom walked Lupe around into the next hallway, "We have a warrant out for you. Why did you come back here to Dayton?"

"I like the city. I have a wonderful new job. I don't ever want to go back to New York City."

"But you must. They have let two of the suspects loose. A third one has been shot and arrested. He shot and wounded your grandmother."

Lupe jumped to attention, "*Mia abuela….*"

He interrupted her, "I'm sorry! How could you have known! Stupid of me! She is fine. She was in the hospital overnight and she is home now and guarded 24 by 7. You do need to go home though."

"Can you wait until this is over and then go with me to Mr. Warner's office? We may need to tell Mr. Slade as well. He is the hospital Administrator."

He looked at her. She looked terrible. Hurt was in her eyes and on her face, "When this class is over, we will go talk to Jim

69

Warner and the administrator. Go sit. I'll tell my Sergeant and he can go with us to the main office." The rest of the two-hour session went smoothly. Lupe fidgeted constantly.

They were sitting outside the chief's office, "That wasn't so bad. The chief understands and Jim Warner understood. And Warner wants you back when you are finished in New York. Hey! Besides all of that, we get to fly. New York City has authorized our tickets."

"I have never been near an airplane."

"Not much different than a train. Not as much room certainly, but sure a lot faster."

The next morning a police car picked up Lupe; Tom was already inside, "Good morning Lupe. We will be at Dayton International shortly. It is not very far." Aunt Bessie waved goodbye from the office window.

As the unmarked police car approached the road marked DEPARTURE there was another large sign:

BIRTHPLACE OF AVIATION

Orville and Wilbur Wright had built their first airplane models here in their bicycle shop.

Lupe was overwhelmed by it all. The terminal was like a giant bus station. Tom led her through the ticketing, the security, and the gate. They boarded first. The Dayton authorities had arranged it. Twenty minutes later they were in the air.

Lupe loved it. She was nervous at first, especially when the plane took-off at full blast; the jet noise was overpowering. It was not a long flight, Lupe had just finished her second cup of Pepsi© when the Captain announced that they were starting to descend and for the flight attendants to cross check and prepare for landing. They were on the ground and at the gate within thirty minutes. It took another fifteen minutes to get their luggage.

Lupe and Tom walked to the waiting NYPD patrol car. He had not handcuffed her. Forty minutes later they were in the same office they had been in eleven weeks before and were talking to Jimmy.

"We'll re-arrest Ladero's two men. We have the third man in custody for shooting your grandmother. He's locked up on an attempt charge. He's got a gunshot wound in his shoulder and won't say how he got it," Jimmy stood up, "His arm is in a sling. Follow me please Miss Guzman."

Ileana was in the next room, her arm was also in a sling, a light blue one. She hugged Lupe as best she could. "Ah! Si! They have brought you. I was so worried of you. They came and got me this morning when they knew you were flying in an *aeroplano* to home."

"I am fine *abuela*. This is Thomas Delano. He is a policeman and a friend from Ohio.'

"I am pleased to meet you *Señor Tomas*."

Jimmy entered, "You may go now. We would like you to stay at your grandmother's until this is over. And we'll have police nearby 24 by 7 so no more shootings."

They dropped all three off at the old building. Tom Delano sat at the small table while Ileana was working with pots and pans in the kitchen of the small flat—with only one arm it was a little difficult.

"Mrs. Montero, why don't you let me order something, they can bring it here. I am sure someone delivers in this neighborhood. You don't need to be cooking with only one usable arm. I have a cell phone."

"Grandma. I will cook. Sit down! Señor Tomas, what would you like? We cook Puerto Rican. We learned it from just being here. The people in this part of the city are mostly from there."

"It doesn't matter. I'll eat just about anything."

Lupe busied herself for the next thirty minutes, finishing what her grandmother had started.

"Dinner is served."

It reminded Tom of the thirty minute cooking show with Rachael Ray. One of the police officers, Marian Shell, back in Dayton, had the TV turned on in the back coffee room all the time. She watched the show when not on patrol and the men had all gotten used to it.

The three sat at the small table. "This is wonderful! Chicken, right?"

"Yes. It is sliced chicken breast rolled in dry breadcrumbs and special seasoning. I cook them in a caldero and use manteca. Lard is not supposed to be good for you, but the flavor is much better."

He forked something else into his mouth, "This tastes like a banana."

"Well sort of. They are bigger. We call them platanas and fry them twice in the caldero. Also in lard."

Lupe rose and brought a covered dish from the cabinet, "Here Tomas, taste these."

Tom tasted one, "This tastes like bananas also."

"These are platanutres or plantain chips."

"If I hang out with you very long, I'll have a lot more to learn I am sure. By the way what is a caldero?"

Lupe was pleased, this was the first time he had indicated that he was going to "hang out with her."

"A caldero is sort of like a skillet or a large steel cooking pan. We call this style of cooking cocina criolla. Creole cooking in English. People who come directly from Spain, like my grandmother, are called pennisulares—someone from the Iberian Peninsula. The next generation, like my Madre, would be a criolla. That is how they named the Puerto Rican cooking."

They finished eating and Tom scooted back his chair, "I ate too much. That was wonderful. By the way, you said you fried the bananas twice. Why?"

"We sear them to seal in the flavor and then dip them in a special glaze and fry them again."

Ileana went to the far cabinet and brought out a dark glass bottle with her good hand, "Tomas, you must have some of this. I only use it for especial times. This is one of those times. It is old and came from Cuba before Castro. It will keep forever." Tom noticed she said Koo-bah for Cuba.

She poured some of the dark amber liquid into three small glasses, "Lupita, you are not old enough, but this is especial, you may have a small glass too." The metalized label was embossed with "Castillo Bacardi."

Lupe thought to herself, *my little grandma is forgetting. I will be twenty-two in August.*

Tom Delano sipped from the small glass, "This is wonderful." He was surprised at how easy the rum went down. He was not a drinker—this was delightful.

They talked for two more hours, Tom looked at his watch, "Time to catch my plane back to Ohio. Passengers have to be there at least two hours ahead of time. We all have to go through the security stuff now since 9/11—even us cops." He arose; Ileana gave him a small hug with her good arm. Lupe wasn't sure what to do.

He turned and embraced Lupe lightly. She was almost embarrassed. Lupe had never been this close to a man before, except on the train when she had fallen asleep—that part she barely remembered. He was taller than she had thought and had strong arms. She had stood by him and walked with him, but just never noticed that he was tall.

Tom bent and picked up his small bag by the door, turned, and said goodbye once more and was gone.

Lupe felt a tug at her heart, *Tomas is really gone*, she said to herself. Her feelings were mixed, "Abuela, what do you think? He is nice, yes?"

"Si. Tomas is nice. What will you do when the police and the courts are done?"

"I will go to Ohio. I have a chance for a wonderful job. Tom is going to the hospital and explain everything to Mr. Warner once again. Mr. Warner has an idea of what I will do here, but Tom will convince him that I will be back for good, I am sure."

"Is he Catholic?"

"*Si.*"

Lupe spent the next twenty minutes telling Ileana about her new job and the chance to make something of her life—and more about Tom. And her new "Aunt" Bessie. And all of the trees. And the river. Lupe rattled on and on—she made it seem exciting.

Ileana wished she were younger. She thought, *I would like this wonderful place called Ohio.*

CHAPTER TWENTY

The arraignment was at the end of October. The trial was in November and would probably last only a day. The two men would surely go to jail for a long time.

The defense lawyers plea-bargained at the last minute and it was all over.

The two men each got eighteen years with a chance of probation. The man who shot her grandmother, Garcia, was sentenced to twenty-five and no chance for probation. The judge had taken into account the fact that he was part of the killing of the two homeless as well as trying to kill Lupe's grandmother.

In a way, Lupe felt relieved; she was now free to go. She thought all three men should have received life. The Judge had been appointed by an earlier regime.

Mikel Andraka had sat in the back of the courtroom all morning and watched both Ileana and Lupe. He followed them outside and stopped Ileana.

"*Señora* I must talk with you once again."

"You are the one who ran after the man from the window. You were just telling me of someone in Spain when the gun was fired."

"*Si.* Yes. I would like to talk more about Spain."

"Come home with us. We can take a bus."

"I have a car. I will drive you." They were home in less than a half an hour. It would have taken Ileana and Lupe almost two hours by bus.

Mikel brought out a photo. He now knew that the search for Carlos was completely innocent.

Ileana looked at the photo, "*Un momento,*" she walked to the cabinet and brought out a box. She fumbled around and brought out a photo of a young man in a German Luftwaffe uniform. He looked just like Carlos.

"Ah *Si!* That man looks just like my *amigo*, Carlos—when Carlos was much younger of course."

Ileana was dumbfounded, "After all of these years, I have found my little *hermano*."

Lupe looked at the photo, "I am sure that he is your brother. Even the ears...," she reached up and pulled her *abuela's* hair back, "....they are shaped just like yours; look at his in the photo." Lupe felt her own ears, "....and mine."

Mikel agreed about the ears and spoke again, "I am flying back to Spain soon. I will tell your brother. He will contact you. When you talk he will have a different name."

Lupe was having a hard time following his quaint Spanish. She couldn't place the accent. Mikel shook hands and soon left.

"Grandma, did you notice the strange Spanish that man, Mikel, was speaking?"

"He is Basque. Let me tell you about the Basque," Ileana spent the next half-hour giving Lupe a history lesson about Basque separatism as she remembered it.

CHAPTER TWENTY-ONE

Lupe stepped from the bus and walked towards the hospital and her new life. She was walking faster and faster, anticipating her first meeting with Mr. Warner and the crew, it had been four weeks and she was tired. The eleven-hour bus ride had been rough. The New York police wouldn't spring for a plane ticket, only the bus. They said as far as they were concerned, she had fled New York City and her home was the city. And they really didn't have to buy her anything.

Mr. Warner looked up when she was escorted into his office by Charlene Moore, a big smile broke on his face, "Come in! Come in! Officer Delano told me the whole story Sally....I mean Lupe. I guess we will all have to get used to your name."

They talked for twenty minutes and then Mr. Warner gave her a stack of papers, "Just cross out Sally Lindstrum and ink in your real name. Initial and date each entry. When you finish give them to Miss Moore and then go report to George. He knows you are back. He has a new badge for you."

He stood up by the window, "And welcome back once more. That young policeman, Tom, likes you. Hang on to him....L..Lupe, he's a good one," he stumbled over her name.

Lupe found George re-packing a medical kit, "Hi George. I'm back."

"I knew. Mr. Warner told me and I saw your cop friend here talking to him the other day, yesterday it was actually. You are just in time. The next session of the classes you missed are starting. You missed six you know. I'm starting over again for the next group."

"You need that many here?" She had a worried look on her face.

"No! No! Two other hospitals are sending people to class. One group is from down in the next county, Warren, and three people from Greene County, none from here, just you. We are the only ones that are offering classes. You can spend extra time and take those six classes. Jim Warner said it was OK. You won't be paid beyond forty hours though."

Lupe was relieved, she could see herself being replaced. Thinking to herself, *why am I so negative?*

She decided it was from living in New York City and living from day to day. This was so much better. She felt good about herself.

George handed her a new badge....Lupe Guzman was printed across the top. She smiled and snapped it on her pocket flap, *this is my third badge in only a few months.*

"Guzman doesn't sound Spanish."

"It anciently comes from a Germanic ancestor when the Visigoths and Goths used to live in Spain. Guzman is a left over name. I looked my last name up in the city library once, back when I was in the eighth grade."

CHAPTER TWENTY-TWO

The three men slipped down the grassy bank and walked towards the pier a quarter of a mile away. They were purposely bent over and Carlos had a hard time keeping them in view. He unpacked his night-glasses and finally spotted them.

He was blinded by a bright set of headlights as the car suddenly appeared around the corner. Carlos stepped back into the bushes on the edge of the scrub coastal forest. He could just barely see that it was a new sedan with halogen lights and not the Guardia Civil.

Carlos could see clearly again after just a moment. The three men were easing themselves into the water near the medium-sized freighter that was bobbing lightly in the swells. It was a calm night and not so much as a gentle breeze. They had picked their target carefully. The freighter was empty and no sailors were on board.

The panel truck was down at the corner below the tall bushes. Carlos would pick up the three men as soon as they signaled. He walked down from the overhang and waited in the truck.

Spanish agent, Pedro Bandolas was also looking through night-glasses. He had lost the three men too. He turned the ignition and drove slowly down the narrow road—only one vehicle at a time, he had noticed. And it was one-way as well. He passed the old panel truck parked in the dirt and weeds and paid no attention. He was concentrating on the location of the men and the ship. He didn't want to miss a moment.

Bandolas stopped at the bottom and shut off the engine. He hadn't turned on the headlights for the last few hundred meters. He had used them only going around the curves above and along the cliffs. Bandolas blinked a small penlight towards a closed café on the waterfront. A blink came back from the corner of the building. It was only thirty meters away.

So the Basques are at it again. I thought maybe the phone call was a hoax. It is true. The man on the other end of the light was a Guardia Civil—a policeman.

Bandolas turned his glasses towards the northwest. Now he saw the three men once more. They were pushing away from the anchored ship. It was an old Greek freighter. The ship was riding high in the water and looked to be empty.

He trained his glasses on the café, *they have spotted the men as well.* The agent wished he had a two-way radio, *I wonder when they will close in?*

Bandolas leaned back in his seat and waited. Gunfire!

He focused the glasses once again. The three men in the water had pulled themselves up onto the bank and were running down the road. The Guardia Civil were firing again. One man was down. Then another. And the third!

Bandolas smiled a worried smile—he was just an observer and he was done observing for the night, *I would not have killed them. I would have saved them for questioning.*

He shook his head as he drove away.

Carlos just sat—stunned!

Where did the police come from? He was sick at heart. These three men were handpicked. He had painfully decided upon them after watching them work for the last six months. They were not exactly what he needed, but he took them on anyway. They had learned well. They were gone!

Two men got out of a police van wearing wet suits. They were in the water in just minutes. Soon one waved a box that had been attached to the ship. Then the other one waved a box and soon a third box. They had found all three boxes. They roped them and pulled them up onto the beach. A bomb squad van took over.

Carlos was disgusted; mostly with himself. He drove slowly away, *I'll have to call a meeting and tell everyone. This has set us back months.*

He was very distraught, *I've lost three more men. Someone had to tell. We have a foreign Spanish spy amongst us.*

He was really discouraged. He kept on. *I screened everyone thoroughly and personally,* he sometimes had them do non-essential espionage acts as a test.

I'm tired and I am getting too old for this stuff. I should give it up before I do something really estupido and lose even more men.

Carlos drove slowly down a dirt road to a cut-off into the mountains. He would be at the hideaway in less than an hour. He watched carefully in the rear-view mirror. No lights were behind him, *this should have been easy tonight. Now I have to find the Spanish spy.*

He drove on until he saw some lights in a little hamlet, "I have only been here once from this direction and that was five years ago." He drove carefully, watching for a turn-off. He saw it. There were fresh tire tracks in the dirt road. There should not have been any tracks. Carlos drove carefully on by and pulled into the next dirt road and parked.

He walked silently back and down the road, following the wide tire tracks. He heard voices speaking softly not far away. Carlos slipped into the brush and crept towards the sounds.

"We have the place surrounded," the man was talking on a radio.

"Si! We will wait until the first cars arrive and move in. We won't get them all, but we will get the leaders.'

Carlos backed out of the brush and carefully walked back to the main road. He looked at his watch. A car was coming. He took a chance. He held up his right hand with the palm out. The car stopped. It was Federico.

"Ah Carlos! Why are you in the road?"

"They have found us out. Where are the others?"

"They are behind us a couple of kilometers or so."

"Turn around and stop them. We will meet tomorrow, back at our usual place. Drive quietly until you are away from here, Adios!"

Carlos walked to his vehicle and carefully drove back towards the hamlet. From there he took a poorly paved road to the southeast, "No sense using the main highways, they may be watching." He took an even smaller, winding foothill road to the left.

"I will tell everyone and watch their reactions. I won't mention that I know there is a spy. I will see for sure. I am slipping. All of these years and I have known who was good and who was not, it is time to stop!"

He thought some more, "I will place Mikel in charge when he returns from America. I am no longer good enough."

Carlos felt his right knee. It hurt. The driving did that, the old bullet wound ached when it rained. It was damp along the seashore. He rubbed it and then lightly pounded on his knee with the flat of his hand. The pain eased. He drove on into the darkness. He had another hour of driving on these poorly maintained mountain roads.

CHAPTER TWENTY-THREE

Lupe carefully wrote down the name of the new textbook. The hospital ordered them at cost and gave one to each student. She would pick it up in the hospital stores office in the basement. George was moving the mouse; a video appeared on the screen. Today's lesson was titled IMMEDIATE ATTENTION.

The nurse in the video was demonstrating the use of the sphygmomanometer. She was using an old-fashioned instrument and was pumping the bulb and listening through a stethoscope. Then she put it aside and used a modern digital one. Lupe had seen the newer type two weeks ago.

George interrupted, "We have three now and have ordered four more for our medical vans. They should be here next week."

Lupe had already seen the digitized unit. Actually she had watched and had written down the data for the instructor representing the manufacturer. The lady had taken six of them through the manual, step-by-step. She carefully printed the long name, sphygmomanometer, in her notes. She would look the word up later in the hospital library; it sounded Greek. She knew a few Greek street words from back in New York.

Tourniquets were next. George handed out copies of various uses of tourniquets, "I copied two of these from an old Boy Scout Handbook. They had better pictures," he laughed.

"Tomorrow we do neck braces and back supports to be used at the scene of an accident." He held up a blue plastic back brace that had been leaning against the table.

The class stopped at eleven. George walked over to Lupe's chair, "The next trip out, I would like you to go along. I know you have been going to the library, but you need more experience. It's a little early in your training, but I have confidence. OK?"

"OK. Thank you George. I will do my very best. I have been staying over at night and making up my time."

"I know. I have seen you. Don't get too tired. Get some sleep. I want my new partner to be wide awake. In fact go home early tonight. I'll sign you out."

"I am going to be your new permanent partner?"

"Yep! I cleared it with Frank Slade."

She grabbed her study bag and walked to her locker. It had a new sign stenciled on the door:

LUPE GUZMAN
MEDICAL EMERGENCY TECHNICIAN

She was so proud. An hour later the buzzer went off in the break room—she ran to the van. George had the motor running. She belted up and they were off. Sandy was in the back.

A sedan had missed the off-ramp turn and lay on its side in the grass. The Ohio highway patrol was already there and had pulled a man the rest of the way out through the broken windshield. He was cut and bleeding profusely.

A few moments later the car burst into flames. A fire truck was coming, they could hear the sirens.

Lupe grabbed the bandage bag and George grabbed the emergency bag. The man only had superficial cuts. The real problem was that he had hit the mirror on his way through the windshield and the mirror and seat belt had cut his stomach and chest as he slipped part way through it. He had been stopped by the windshield wiper mechanism when his belt was caught in it. He was bleeding and incoherent.

Lupe talked to him incessantly. He focused on her voice and stayed awake. He made a soft cooing sound—almost a moan.

George used a light and looked into his eyes, "I think he has concussion. He hit his head hard as he slid through. Let's get him moved into the van and back to the trauma center."

"NOW! STAT!" He yelled.

He and Lupe picked up the stretcher on the count of two; a police officer opened the double doors in back. They loaded the man inside and they were off. Lupe stayed in the back with him and monitored his heart and blood pressure. The second van crew took over the scene.

"George! His pressure is dropping."

"We are almost there. Raise his feet and legs higher if you can. We are six minutes away. They are waiting for us." They pulled in under the overhang, an orderly jerked the door open and they had the man out in seconds.

Lupe checked back forty minutes later. The man had been stabilized, bandaged, and moved down the hallway—waiting for a room.

Lupe spotted him and walked towards him. He looked up at her and smiled. She stayed a moment longer. He dozed off. They had given him benadryl. He didn't have concussion after all, just a bad bump. He was going to have a bad headache for a few days. They had patched the cuts on his chest and left arm, he was breathing normally.

George walked by Mr. Warner's office and peeked in through his open door, "We picked a good one. That Lupe's great. Tell Slade when you see him," he held his thumb upright and walked away.

Mr. Warner smiled and looked down at the budget report he had been reading, *what a great emergency staff the hospital had.*

He liked being in charge of Human Resources, especially when there was a success. The report was very detailed. They needed two more registered nurses and they were still short a cleaning person.

CHAPTER TWENTY-FOUR

He stopped. "Padre! I found you. What are you doing way out here?"

"I have found these young trees and they needed trimming. I rarely come here in the back lot. The brush is growing up too. I must find someone in the village to do this work."

"I need a favor. Let's find a place to sit for a while. And Padre, I will find you someone for the trees."

They moved to a flat rock that had been placed for just that purpose a few centuries ago. It had not been used much lately, it was covered in patina and green moss was thick on the north side.

"What can I do for you my son?"

"I need to find out if my real mother came here before I was born? I know that she died shortly afterwards. My stepmother said my mother was able to walk a little before the infection weakened her. And would there be any papers? Perhaps a baptismal record or something?"

"I would not think so. Si, I remember when you told me once that you were adopted and that your biological Madre had died. Perhaps someone did bring a paper of some kind after she was gone. I have papers under your name now. I have hidden them in my desk. What was your real name or do you know?"

Si. I know my name. Karl Hirschmann. That is Karl with a K in the spelling."

"I cannot look this afternoon. I have a mass later. I will look in the archives. Padre Benedicto, who was here before me, was very good. He was good at indexing. He spent much time; hours and days in the basement archives. Our *Obispo* said too much time."

"Gracias Padre. Gracias. And Bishops are always right." He smiled when he said it.

"Why do you need this my son?"

"I am thinking of going away. I am getting older. And careless. I lost some men last week."

"I heard. I am Basque too, but I do not think I could do such things. It was a sad loss."

"We have never killed anyone in all these years, Padre."

"*Si.* I know. But there may come a time. The new government is pushing hard to stop you. The Spanish government has conceded some things in the last few years. We have our own State."

"We want to be a country and not part of Spain. We Basques were here first—for countless centuries before the Romans and the Spanish and the French. We are an ancient people."

"Carlos, I will let you know what I find. I must go to the marketplace on Thursday. I will meet you there. We will have a noontime meal. Perhaps some wine, bread, cheese; we will think of something that will help you."

They both rose from the rock seat and Carlos headed for his parked van.

The padre turned and yelled, "You must come to Mass!" The Padre thought to himself, *poor Carlos. Being adopted is wonderful, but not always rewarding. His reward will be later. He has fought hard for us Basques although it seems that he is not one. Even so he is one of us in his heart.*

The Padre headed for his little alcove office; he had to write some words for this evening. A small family group was coming to talk with him. Their son was in trouble. He was being held in a Spanish jail and the parents and siblings were worried.

I wonder where Carlos was going, why would he need the old papers?

The Padre was getting old too. This was his third, and probably his last, Church, *sadly my flock is diminishing. People were not coming to Church like they used to do. There are exceptions. Two of the former soldiers that were in the Iraq War, lived in the village; they came to mass every Sunday. The war with the Muslims has changed them.* He often thought of the historical Muslim Moors. They controlled Spain for almost six hundred years.

To himself, *do we need a war or a disaster to cause people to come to Church?*

The Padre hoped not! *And this is such a wonderful old Church. Why would anyone not want to come?*

He loved the beautiful colors of the leaded glass.

I will say a special prayer for Carlos Elazar Cados—Karl Hirschmann—tonight.

CHAPTER TWENTY-FIVE

Two of Ladero's men drove slowly past the old tenement. There was a cop car parked across the street and one in the alley.

"Ladero said he wanted this *rubia* killed even though she has already testified. We need to find her for him."

"Nobody has seen this *rubia* for a long time."

Mikel strolled around the corner. He was going to say goodbye to Eleana and catch the next plane for Madrid. He saw the car with the broken antenna, driving slowly by, and he saw the cops in the alley. Someone in the gang must have recovered the car from the police impound lot. He carefully turned and sauntered down the sidewalk, staying in the shadows and hoping the car would turn left.

It did.

Mikel walked swiftly behind it. The light turned red. He moved to the car and placed the gun with the silencer in the open window and spoke in his quaint Spanish, "Unlock the back door."

Click! Mikel jumped in back, still pointing the gun at the driver, "Go down the block and turn into Standard Street. Pull into the alley behind the green painted store."

The driver parked behind the green store and turned in his seat, he was reaching for his pistol inside his jacket. The other passenger pulled a switchblade.

Mikel fired point blank and then shot the other one who had started to pull the knife. He pushed them out into the rubbish, hopped in behind the wheel, and drove to a numbered street.

He parked the car two miles away and carefully wiped the steering wheel and door handles; he again remembered the American passion for fingerprints. He wiped his face with the same cloth. Small splashes of blood had hit him. He tossed the dirty cloth inside. It landed on the floor—passenger side.

He left the keys in the ignition, *somebody will probably steal it.* He had seen that on TV as well. Auto theft was a big business in America—chop shops they called them. Mikel shook his head, *such a place.*

He walked four blocks, ducked into an alley, shed his stained jacket, threw the gun into a trash bin after wiping it clean, and hailed a passing cab. It had only taken fifteen minutes.

Three hours later he was on a British Air MD-11 flight to Madrid, by way of London. Without reservations, it was the only flight with an open Business Class seat and with a connection on to Madrid.

Ileana and Lupe will be safe now. Carlos will be pleased. These two worked for the jefe. He knew that everyone had to have a boss of some kind. Mikel finished the red wine the attendant had brought him, tilted the Business Class seat all the way back, and was soon asleep.

"Jimmy! We found two of Scippio Ladero's men dumped in an alley. They were shot at close range gang style—in the back of the head."

"OK. We'll look into it, but not too hard. No great loss. We have other more important things to do."

The older Iberian Air passenger plane from London, droned on towards Madrid. Mikel had slept almost all the way from New York to London.

He was at peace and he could tell Carlos that he had found his sister and it was safe for him to go to America. He felt rested. He thought about plans for the next raid, *I will be the jefe aqui--now.*

CHAPTER TWENTY-SIX

The Padre brushed the dust off the bottom of his black frock. He had been in the basement for three hours. He had two yellowed papers in his left hand, *I will meet Carlos for lunch. He will be pleased.* He ran copies of the papers. It was nice and cozy in his little office; he fell asleep in his old swivel chair.

The market place was crowded. Carlos spotted the Padre. The black frock stood out, *"Buenas dias Padre!"*

"Ah. *Si.* Hello. I have something for you. First let's get something to eat. I am hungry."

They were soon seated in the shade of a small tree in the center of the plaza, "I have found some papers. Perhaps these will help," he handed them to Carlos.

The Padre shared a large sandwich with Carlos and each had bought a glass of wine. They were almost silent while eating.

Carlos looked at the papers. "Yes. There is my mother's name. Here is my father's name. I am indeed a Hirschmann—a German. The Civil War was on and the Basques helped the Communist. The Communists made a promise and then couldn't keep it. They lost."

"Carlos my son. Are you sure that you need to do this move now?"

"Padre, I am going to stop this fighting. I am no longer alert enough to do these things. The last three operations have gone wrong. It is time for me to retire."

"Where will you go?"

"It depends upon what Mikel has found in America. If it is a good thing, I will go seek my sister. I have never seen her to remember. I always knew I had one though."

"Ah! I will miss you. And so will the children that you have helped. But you have need to find your *hermana* in America and I understand. It is time. That will be a good thing. May you go with God!"

They shook hands and the Padre raised his hand and made a sign over Carlos. They went in different ways.

The cell phone rang. It was Mikel, "I will see you at our meeting place," and clicked off.

Twenty minutes later they were at the bar. Mikel quietly told Carlos everything.

"I must go to America. What will I need?"

"I know all the paperwork. I will have it ready. How will you be known? Not Carlos. You are dead."

Carlos handed Mikel the two papers the Padre had found, "Will these work?"

"*Si*. These are wonderful. I can have papers in less than two weeks. You will enter under Karl Hirschmann and then you will be given another set of papers in America. You will have a different name. *Adios*. I must start right away. The office is still open if I drive fast. It is only fifty kilometers. You remain quiet. You need only appear two days before you leave. I will also arrange for tickets."

"Oh! And Carlos, you will need about four-thousand Euro-dollars for this."

Mikel was excited. He would soon be in charge. He had some wonderful new ideas; he would blow up a bridge. One leading into the Pyrenees, *it'll keep those foreign Spanish out of Basque lands for a month or two anyway. At least a little piece of our homeland or a little peace in our homeland.* He laughed at his word play.

He loved Carlos, he was like a father to him, but he wanted to do things differently. He would make a heavy mark on the foreign Spanish. He could feel it. He smiled for two or three kilometers—thinking.

Carlos waited a few minutes until Mikel was out of sight, walked to his parked van, and then drove back to the farmhouse where he was temporarily staying.

He thought, *what a life, I have nothing to take care of, my bank account is almost empty. I have no home of my own. This is not even my car. Sixty some years old and I only have a few clothes and some old Spanish Civil War papers that belonged to my mother and father.*

Karl Hirschmann shook his head and drove on. America was suddenly appealing to him. The name Hirschmann suddenly seemed right. Carlos really was dead.

And then he remembered something, *in 1967 a strange little man from Zurich had found him and knocked on the door. Carlos was staying with a friend in San Sebastian, they had been coordinating with the French Basques.*

The man spoke French, but not Spanish. Luckily Carlos understood some French. It seems that the grandfather in Germany had passed away. He left a sum of money to his only descendants—Erik Hirschmann's children.

At the time Carlos was not interested. He signed the papers and told the man from Zurich to just leave it in the bank, he was too busy to worry about it right now. The little man never said how he knew where to find Carlos.

I had completely forgotten about it until just now. That was over forty years ago. I wonder how much it was? I never bothered to ask. I was too busy plotting against the foreign Spanish.

CHAPTER TWENTY-SEVEN

The plane landed smoothly at Kennedy. Karl Hirschmann was through customs in less than an hour. He only had a carry-on bag and a small 1960's style suitcase. There would be a small amount of his money in a bank. Mikel had arranged it somehow. Carlos—Karl—didn't want to know. His papers looked very good, especially the yellowed baptismal paper the Padre had found for him. The Padre had made a copy and placed the copies in the archives.

A taxi took him to the address in Spanish Harlem where his sister lived. He found her third floor door and knocked.

Ileana knew immediately; she rushed into his arms and hugged him. Then she kissed his cheek. Karl didn't know what to do. *What does a lifetime warrior do?* Finally he hugged her back and gently kissed her forehead.

"Oh my *hermano*, we have a lot to discuss."

"Ah. *Si.* We do."

Ileana immediately got out the old pictures. They sat on the old sofa. "Here is a photo of your father. He is handsome like you Karl, you are half German."

"I have been raised as a Basque."

He proceeded to tell her of that part of his life working in the Basque ETA, trying to force Spain to give them sovereignty. Mostly pecking away at them and constantly wearing them down.

Ileana understood.

Ileana showed him some photos of his mother when she was a child. Karl was visibly moved. He had wondered about his parents when he was younger, but had put those thoughts out of his memory when he started with the ETA. The ETA had become his family.

His stepparents had moved to the little town of Villa Belon. It was only twenty kilometers from his birthplace near the Spanish airfield built for the Luftwaffe. His stepfather had become part of the ETA and Karl followed him shortly after he was fifteen.

Now that he was a few decades older, Karl was suddenly interested in the family. Ileana had forced the childhood memories to come back; the harshness of the mountains; the grazing of the skinny sheep; the Spanish; and the wonderful comfort when they had moved to Villa Belon. There was no electricity, no running water, and no heat other than a fireplace and a stove in the kitchen, but it was far far above the conditions he had lived under on the dry plains below the Pyrenees.

Karl looked at a photo of a little girl, "Who is this?'

"That is me when I lived with my Tia, I mean our aunt. She was yours too."

"I never knew of any of my mother's family. I have some old papers dating from 1936 to 1941—they end on that date. I'll dig them out of my *bolsa* and let you read them. I left it and my clothes in the small hotel down the street, El Mar."

He thought for a moment, "One of the leather handles came loose on the trip. I must fix it. And this very pretty girl. Who is she?"

"That is my granddaughter, Lupe. She is in Ohio and works in a *grande* hospital. She is very smart."

"Ah. *Si.* She looks like you; a rubia. So I am a *Tio. Tio* Karl. A *grande* uncle."

"And looks like you too Karl. She has our ears and hair," she unconsciously felt her hair and pushed a graying sprig back.

Karl continued, "Yes. It has been my bane. It is hard to hide in a crowd. I often died my hair." Karl rose, "I must go. I have to meet an old friend. He is to help me to stay in America."

"That is wonderful. My own *hermano* in America. Perhaps we can go to Ohio. Lupe was my only relative, now Karl, I have two."

"We shall see. I will be back in a few days. Do not worry for me. I have a few things to do. I will be called differently too when I come back."

CHAPTER TWENTY-EIGHT

Mikel watched each man carefully. The fifteen men filed in and took their regular seats around the long oval table. Carlos had warned him. He was looking at each man with veiled suspicion. The three empty chairs were conspicuous. And the seat Mikel was sitting in seemed odd to the group. Carlos had sat there for so many years. The seat next to him was also empty, Mikel's old seat.

Mikel had known Pedro for many years. Gorge had been with them for ten. He had watched the rest straggle in, Ander, Gotzon, Palben, Xabier, and Danel. Palben was blond like his Basque name. The others coming in now, were newer, but had been with them for at least three years.

Mikel was concerned. *He knew them all, how will I know? Something must give the Spanish spy away*. He thought of each one again and the part they had played in their attempt at blowing up the old freighter in the harbor.

Where was each man? Who had left the meeting room last? Who might have called the Guardia Civil? These were all rhetorical questions and Mikel had no answers.

They met and planned for almost four hours, "We must leave. There is a banquet in this room and Señor Calaveras wants to clean up and put on clean tablecloths. This banquet event is scheduled once a year and we cannot change it. We must leave."

Mikel walked to the south end of the second floor. He was looking for Juan Calaveras—he found him, "We are leaving. You may clean up."

"Ah! Gracias. Will Palben want to use my phone again? If so I will leave my door unlocked."

Mikel blinked and turned. Startled for just a second, "No. He will not need it tonight. Do I owe anything for the phone calls? Let's see how many were there? Three I think."

"No. It is fine. There were four, one after each meeting. He said he was calling his wife."

"Ok. That is *bueno*!"

Gotzon was picking up his car keys; he had left them on the bar downstairs. Mikel caught up with him.

"Gotzon, I must talk with you. Let us walk out onto the portico."

"We have a Spanish spy. Palben has made a call after each of the last four meetings to his wife. Funny thing, he has never been married. You know what to do."

"*Si*. And goodnight," he walked towards his car.

"*Si, buenos tardes.*"

A week later a badly damaged body, with blond hair, washed up on the beach, it was on French soil. The Gendarmes thought the man was a German, there were no clothes and no unusual markings on the body, just normal damage from the sea and sea creatures. Three teeth had been deliberately knocked out. The police figured the fillings might have identified the man. The case folder was put in a file drawer—towards the back.

A week later, Gotzon met Mikel at a bar; he rolled three teeth towards Mikel, drank his drink, never said a word, and left by the alley door.

Mikel picked them up, he would save them as a reminder. Two had gold fillings, the third was all gold. He thought about it for a moment. He tossed the two filled teeth into the trashcan behind the bar counter and placed the gold one in his pocket— three was bad luck to a Basque.

CHAPTER TWENTY-NINE

Lupe was looking through the Sinclair College brochure that was on the counter in the emergency room. They offered an EMS certificate. She thought to herself, *I am doing emergency response work now. Maybe emergency medical service is a class I would need.*

She looked at the map on the back, the community college was just off Perry and the parking lot was on Fourth Street, *I know exactly where that is. Maybe I'll stop into the admissions office tonight after work. I can follow the Great Miami River walk. I'll ask Mr. Warner first though,* she was taking driving lessons. Walking would soon be a thing of the past, if only she could find a decent used car.

Lupe jerked when the speaker blared. George was already running for the medical van. She grabbed the small red bag and ran after him. He had been watching the monitor in the corner. A warning came on the monitor first and then the speakers 25 seconds later. The coffee break room had a loud buzzer that started up at the same time.

The second outside set of double doors automatically opened and stayed open anytime the emergency system was activated. The van headed for the river bridge.

Lupe eyed the bandage bag. It was within easy grasp on the floor in front of her. She still had the red emergency bag on her lap. The van careened around the curve along the riverbank. George turned onto the small road leading to the bridge. They could see flames and smoke at the other end.

Lupe was anxious, it looked bad. She had never seen flames coming from a burning auto that were this high. It exploded. The gasoline splattered in ignited globs. Some car broken parts sizzled in the river water.

George rushed in and Lupe was right behind him. They managed to pull just one person out, a little girl. Actually she had been thrown almost clear. Evidently she had not been wearing her seat belt. They carried her back to the van and the flaming car blew again. The car was now totally engulfed in flames. The little girl was not aware of anything; she was unconscious.

A patrolman walked over where Lupe and George were attending to the little girl, "As near as we can tell the occupants were from Sweden. This was a Hertz rental car. Mr. and Mrs. Olaf Vendaulf and child. They were here on vacation and business, so the paperwork at the rental office says. I just talked to them on the phone."

He then read from a paper that had been printed out from the machine in the van, "This is from Hertz in Cleveland. It says that Vendaulf was a parts purchasing agent for Volvo. He was here visiting TRW Automotive in Cleveland, Ohio. He comes to America often and they know him well at Hertz in Cleveland."

The little eight-year old awakened and started crying, "I'll take her," Lupe led the little girl to the emergency van. She was blond like Lupe. She sat her on her lap, "What's your name?"

The little girl shook her head, "I'm Lupe," and Lupe pointed at herself.

"Um! Noora Rebeka," and she pointed at herself. She said her name in a sing-song accent. Lupe smiled and continued trying to communicate with the little girl.

George was finished, "C'mon Lupe. We'll take her back to the hospital until the authorities figure out what to do with her. The cops said we could go. I want to check her over for cuts and scratches and then have a doctor look at her."

They loaded up their equipment and drove away. Noora sat on her lap. Lupe fastened the long seat belt around both of them.

CHAPTER THIRTY

The second day, Ileana showed Karl where she worked. He looked around, noticing the neighborhood. He could tell that this was a poorer section of the city. It was fairly clean—only poor. He remembered the money the little man from Zurich had him sign for, tomorrow he would find a bank. He wondered again how much money; it had been there for over forty years; always compounding. He had the Zurich bank account number on a slip of paper packed away in his leather *bolsa.*

Karl slept on Lupe's cot. It was sagging a bit from his weight, but not bad. He woke up just as the sun peeked through the crevasse generated by the two taller buildings on the east side of the street. It reminded him of the last time he had been in Madrid nine years ago. He had slept on a cot at a friend's house. Both the Guardia Civil and the Army were looking for him. The sun had crept into the room in the same way as this morning.

He washed and shaved. He had shaved his mustache off for the passport photo. He was growing his mustache back, *I won't look like my passport, but I won't need it ever again anyway.*

He thought perhaps he should throw it away. It was false. All he needed was to be caught with a fake passport. The US Customs computer had probably flagged him by now. He ripped it up and trashed it.

He laughed, *the Americans wait until a plane is airborne before they publish the passenger list, not the most inteligente thing to do.*

Ah! My new identity papers, I almost forgot, he retrieved an insertion razor blade from the kit and broke the plastic holder, there were three tiny blades embedded in the head. With one of the flimsy blades he slit the liner in his shaving kit. There was a folded paper and a small card inside. He trashed the three sharp slivers of steel and the broken plastic holder.

He read the small folded note, "This is your new birth certificate. Roberto Sanchez. You were born in Bernalillo, New Mexico." It had been chemically weathered and looked as old as the sixty odd years that he was. It also listed his three middle names. One was obviously the mother's maiden name, Lopez.

There was a social security card in the slit as well. The card was real and so was the name, but another Roberto Sanchez. It looked old too. This other Roberto was born in San Martin, Mexico, had worked in Los Angeles, and then disappeared eighteen years ago.

The man who had sold the papers had made sure that the social security office listed him as from New Mexico. The man had paid a government clerk considerable money. The note that the two papers were wrapped in, also said to read it and then burn it. The social security card was wrinkled and a little smudged, *this will be good.*

It had cost over four thousand dollars for both the certificate and the social security card. The seller, a Basque, had guaranteed that neither of the two Roberto Sanchez's would ever show up and that their records were clean.

Ho Kay Roberto Sanchez, you are alive again. I will tell my sister the new name. The new Roberto folded the certificate and placed both into his new wallet. He emptied the waste can into a grocery store plastic bag, "I will dump this myself on the way outside."

CHAPTER THIRTY-ONE

The Hospital administrator was looking for Lupe. He finally found her, "Lupe! Do you have a moment? I would like to talk with you."

"Yes I do. I'm on my break. What can I do?"

"Do you remember the little Swedish girl that was in the burning car?"

"Yes."

"It seems that there are no relatives. Her father was an only child and his parents, her grandparents, are dead. The mother came from Finland and is of Swedish ancestry, but they can't seem to locate any relatives in the Helsinki records office. The social workers here are in a quandary. She won't try talk to them and she keeps asking for you—Loo-pay."

"Oh my! What can I do?"

"Would you take care of her for a week while the authorities in Sweden try and find an aunt or uncle or someone. The little girl won't eat either. Take a few days off. We'll see that you are paid. In a way this is an emergency." He smiled a rare smile.

"I could, but I have three more days of class. I am making the classes up as it is."

"Perhaps you can bring her here. I am sure she can play in the hospital playroom. It is reserved for children with cancer and blood disorders, but she is young and probably won't even notice that some are bald. It would be good for her and them too I think. They have a puppy too. The little dog gets to spend two hours with the children each day."

"OK. I will do my best. I'll talk to my landlord, Aunt Bessie. I am sure she won't mind. She loves children."

So Noora moved in. It was a challenge at first. They struggled for two days. Even a drink of water was difficult. The girl would point and Lupe would try and follow her finger. It didn't always work.

Finally Lupe decided it was time for the little girl to learn some basic English words. She bought a cheap child's "white board" and some erasable pens of different colors. The board was no bigger than a large paper tablet, but it would do.

She started out just as she had done years ago in Kindergarten and First Grade: CAT—DOG—COW—GIRL—BOY—RUN—SLEEP—STOP—WALK and so on. By the end of the week they were making small sentences. Lupe learned *flicka* for girl and a few other simple Swedish words.

George was upset at first, but he calmed down and let Lupe come in a few minutes late, take a longer lunch, and leave early. He too felt sorry for the little girl. No parents and no relatives. Aunt Bessie didn't mind; she loved it.

After three weeks, Noora and Lupe were talking about everything. She had finally told her about her parents and Noora had cried herself to sleep.

School was going to start soon. Lupe figured out that Noora would be the equivalent to the third grade here in Ohio. She wondered if the Swedish authorities were making any progress, *I will take her to school next week and enroll her. I am sure Tomas will help me.*

Tom did, he wore his uniform. The filing out of the forms went like clockwork. The tall uniformed officer intimidated the young admissions clerk.

Noora was to start on Monday.

CHAPTER THIRTY-TWO

The front door was ajar; Tom Delano stepped inside. He saw the landlord at her desk, "I would like to speak to Lupe Guzman. Can you ring her please or do you have to go get her?"

He had a small bouquet of flowers in his hand.

"I'll get her. She has told me about you. You are the policeman that took her to New York—twice!" She smiled a mischievous smile.

He didn't say anything, but he could tell she was joking with him. Aunt Bessie went to find Lupe.

"Hello Tomas. What brings you here?"

He brought the flowers from behind his back and held them out, "These are for you. I would like to take you to dinner tonight. This is your day off. I found that out at the hospital." He liked her calling him Tomas.

Lupe looked at him not sure what to say.

Bessie spoke first, "Lupe let me take the flowers for you. I'll put them in some water. They are very pretty Officer Delano. Lupe, I will watch Noora."

"Yes. *Si*. They are. Thank you Tomas."

"You are welcome. Now what do you say. Dinner? Where would you like to go? Or shall I pick?"

"I will go. You pick a place. I do not know the town that well. Let me change clothes quickly. I'll be right back."

"OK. You won't be sorry. We are going to the Stockyards Inn on Third. It has been here a long time and is excellent. You will get a taste of Midwestern cooking. If you were a year or two older, a nice wine as well. Instead you get sparkling wine—white grape juice that looks like Champagne. Remember you are dinning with a cop." He laughed.

Aunt Bessie had a large smile on her face, "I've been listening. Noora will be just fine while you are gone. She is watching TV in the other room anyway and I'll fix her a grilled cheese sandwich. She will have to learn to eat American food someday. Hurry! Get out of here."

"I'll be back in a couple of hours. Goodbye."

She turned to Tom, "I am over 21."

CHAPTER THIRTY-THREE

The car drove well. It was three years old, but had low mileage. Roberto Sanchez had made a good deal. His sister was nodding and almost asleep. The trunk was full, the back seat was full, and a small rack, temporarily fastened to the car roof, was stacked with cardboard boxes of clothes. He had covered the boxes with a blue plastic tarp. It had rained twice since they had left New York.

He looked at the map again as he drove. The dashboard was heaped in maps.

Ah, Columbus is ahead. Must be named after Spain's famous explorer. Time to stop for the night. I am tired and Ileana is almost asleep.

He pulled over at a motel that had a flashing vacancy sign. It looked nice. There was even a swimming pool. He would rent a room with two beds.

Ileana came awake when they stopped, "What is this place Karl?"

"Call me Roberto. Please remember. This is a motel as you call them, an inn—*la fonda* in Spain. We will sleep and start again in the morning. Are you hungry?"

"*Si*. Both. I am sleepy and hungry." They ate at the nearby truckers' café and slept until almost seven o'clock the next morning.

"Time to go. We may be able to make Dayton in a couple of hours it is less than 80 miles. I think that is 130 kilometers. I must get used to the measures in this country. After all I am supposed to be from New Mexico. I need to buy some *gasolina*."

"Roberto, Lupe will be surprised. She does not know we are coming."

"And she knows not much of me. This is a nice car. She will be surprised. Would you really like to surprise her even more?"

"Why do you ask such a question?"

"I have a lot of money, it was left to us by our grandfather in Germany. I paid no attention. It was in a Swiss bank for over forty years collecting interest. I will buy a house in this place called Dayton. Then we will find Lupe. She will be surprised. Half is yours. He was your grandfather too."

"We have no furniture, no beds, no chairs, no nothing."

"I will buy it all. I have over a million in Americano money in a bank. With this many Americano dollars, a merchant will no trouble to bending backwards selling us what we need."

"OK. We'll do it. We will really surprise Lupe. And that is bending over backwards," she laughed.

"We will look in the newspapers. They must have a house we would like."

Two hours later they were on the outskirts of Dayton. They saw a real estate office just as they turned off at a ramp that had a hospital sign.

"Let's stop in and ask about homes."

An agent met them at the door. He had just placed the OPEN sign in the door's window. He had been watching as they got out of the car. Business was slow and he was anxious. His broker was out in the west end of the city talking with a subdivision superintendent. The broker wanted to be the first to place a few of his salesmen in the tract sales office.

"Good morning folks. Looking for a house? We got plenty of them. Where abouts in town?"

"Good morning. We are looking, near the hospital where my granddaughter works. I forgot the name."

"Here's a map, show me."

Ileana looked at the arrow where they were now and she looked in all directions, saw an open space with a hospital in the center, "*Aqi*, that is the place. I recognize the name now."

"How close would you need to be? I have nice homes to the west."

"I would think twenty-five blocks."

"Blocks? Where are you folks from? We use miles out here or sometimes minutes."

"New York City, she thought for a moment, "OK! Three or four miles would be good."

"Let me show you some listings out west of the Miami Valley Golf course and south of McKinley, that's Fort McKinley, we tend to shorten the name."

"Point to that please."

"Right here. How much would you want to spend?"

"We have no idea. Show us some prices and the house that goes with them."

The agent was almost wringing his hands in glee, but he restrained himself. He had a couple of bumpkins for clients, "Here is one with four bedrooms, a basement, three bathrooms, and a double garage. You'll need to buy a riding lawnmower though; it has a big backyard. Both a damage/repair expert and a termite company have inspected the property. It's free of both—damage and termites."

"Ileana turned to "Roberto" and winked. He got it. The sales guy was a greedy jerk. He had never dealt with a New Yorker or a Basque.

Three hours later they had bought a new home. The agent wasn't smiling such a big smile. They had made an offer and the seller had taken it. It was ninety-five thousand less than the original price.

The seller had been promoted to a vice-president and had to move to the company headquarters in Chicago. The big house had been on the market for over five months. He needed the cash. The house had been empty for three months.

"When can we move in?"

"As soon as we can set up your credit. How much down payment do you plan to put into escrow?"

"Cash!"

"Cash?"

"Yes, cash. Now how soon?"

"It's early. The banks are just opening. I'll talk to the escrow office. I am sure they will work this rapidly. We have been dealing with them for over a decade." he rushed to the phone. Ileana and Roberto waited in the office lobby and had a cup of instant coffee.

"What is this stuff?"

"It is called instant coffee."

"I could give it another name," he poured it out into a green plant sitting by the window.

Ileana smiled, "That is not a real plant Roberto."

He laughed for the first time in many years, "It will grow new paper leaves after absorbing that awful stuff."

Two hours later they were shopping for furniture in the Bombay store, it had everything; beds, living room furniture, kitchen utensils, and TVs. Roberto spent fifteen thousand dollars and they were to deliver it that day before 4:00 o'clock.

The house was completely set up by four. Lupe got off work at five. Roberto and Ileana waited outside the emergency doors of the hospital. They saw Lupe before she saw them.

"Lupe! Lupita!"

"Grandma. What are you doing here?" She was shocked.

"We came to visit. Get in the back. This is my *hermano*, Roberto, your great uncle."

"After all of these years you have found him. That is wonderful grandma. I am so pleased to meet you," she stuck out her hand—on impulse he reached back over the seat and gave her an awkward hug.

Lupe was puzzled. Her grandmother had called him Roberto. She would ask when they were alone.

They drove west towards the golf course. Roberto pulled into a circular drive and parked in front of four white columns holding up a peaked porch roof similar to a plantation in the Old South.

"Come inside Lupe."

She followed them, "What is this place? Who owns it? Does the owner know we are here?"

"We own it. My brother and I bought it this morning."

Lupe just looked at the both of them. Dumfounded!

CHAPTER THIRTY-FOUR

It was nice outside. "Tom, I had a wonderful time. You were right the food was excellent. Some things I had never eaten before. The sweet potatoes for instance. We never had them in New York. I know what they are. You can buy them in Harlem markets."

"I am glad. We'll do it again, only in another place. I know of several more," he drove slowly towards her rooming house and walked her to the front door. Aunt Bessie had turned on a nightlight—it was late and she had gone to bed. Tom turned Lupe towards him and kissed her. She was surprised, but not displeased.

"Goodnight Lupe."

"Goodnight," she turned and went down the hall. A look of wonderment on her face; she was in a daze. Had Tom really kissed her, she touched her lips. She wandered down the hall. This was her last night here. Tomorrow she moved in with her grandmother and great uncle Roberto. She had forgotten to ask about his name.

The next morning was a day off. She packed her few belongings, went to the front and told Aunt Bessie goodbye, "I will come and see you often. We will have lunch up the street like we did those other days."

"I understand. I would like to meet your grandmother, she sounds like a wonderful lady. And your uncle too."

"You must come over. I will fix Puerto Rico style food. I'll let you know. It will be shortly after we are settled in.

"Goodbye again," her uncle Roberto pulled up and stood outside the car door.

Lupe carried most of her loose things under one arm and the Army duffel bag was strapped around her shoulder and a box, tied with string, was in her right hand. Roberto opened the trunk. They left quietly. He and Ileana had picked up Noora the day before just after her school had let out for the day.

"This will be your room. It has its own bathroom with a tub and a shower."

"It is wonderful. Only the hotels where I carried bags had rooms as nice as this. This is better really. I love it already."

Noora had taken the smaller room across the hall. Her English was vastly improving and she was resigned to the death of her parents—she loved Lupe.

Roberto bought a riding John Deere lawnmower and was having the time of his life playing big estate owner. He mowed the grass more than he should. He was afraid he had killed it. A rain came and it was green overnight. He needed to mow it again.

Lupe was floating in the clouds. She had her grandmother with her. She had an uncle she had only heard about. She had a new room, a 'new' little sister, and a wonderful boyfriend. Tom came by the hospital at least twice a week just to say hello.

They had tried two more nice restaurants, one was Mexican and the other was a German restaurant. There were a lot of Germans in Ohio she had found. She liked the German restaurant. Tom had said that it must be inherited and laughed. They had talked and talked at each place after the meal. One waitress gave them funny looks, until Tom left a large tip, then she was all smiles.

Tom found a Swedish restaurant and they took Noora along. She talked to one of the owners who used to live in Gothenburg. Noora told him she was from there and that her father worked for Volvo.

Lupe finished the classes at the hospital and had enrolled at Sinclair. She was doing well. The college had waived the requirement of her high school transcript in New York. Mr. Warner had a lot to do with it.

Lupe was still a little afraid of Scippio's gang; although the police had assured her that everything was fine. She would finish the EMS class in eighteen months and receive a certificate.

Life was good! Nothing more could go wrong. Noora had been with her a month and Lupe still only worked part time at the hospital. The Swedish government had given up on finding Noora's relatives. A judge gave Lupe temporary custody under the sponsorship and direction of the hospital administrator and senior staff.

CHAPTER THIRTY-FIVE

The airplane from New York landed smoothly. Eduardo Palvi picked up his bag from the carousel at the Dayton International Airport. He spotted the Hertz counter at the end of the long open hall. His car was ready—a four-door Toyota.

He pulled a folded map out of his pocket studied it for a moment, and was on the road to the main part of Dayton in less than ten minutes after arriving. He was to meet a man at the Squires Motel at 6:00 o'clock. He looked at his watch. He had forty minutes.

Eduardo found the motel fifteen minutes early. There was only one car parked in the row, and a man was waiting in front of A-12. Eduardo spoke to the man in Spanish.

"*Si.* Let's go into the room," the man had a small leather bag.

"OK. Let's see what you have. Scippio said you were good."

"I have a 9 mm. The number has been filed off. Here are two boxes of ammo and a shoulder holster. Here is the good digital camera you ordered and a pair of night-glasses. They are a copy of Army issue. A can of chloroform as you asked. Here is the address of the hospital and also where she lives. Now the money."

Not knowing any differently, he had given Eduardo, Lupe's old room address.

Eduardo peeled off twelve hundred dollar bills, "Here. This is the remaining sum that was agreed upon."

"*Si. Adios.* We will not meet. I have no place here in Dayton. I live somewhere else. Have a good night's rest." Eduardo closed the door.

The next day Eduardo drove by the hospital, looking at all of the side streets and the closeness of expressway exits. He followed the river for two miles and then backtracked. He found Lupe's rooming house. He parked across the street and noticed who went in and who went out.

He went back to the hospital and waited in the back lot. He noticed when the most workers left for the day and when the new ones came on shift. He looked for the *rubia*. He didn't see her in the crowd.

The next afternoon he waited down the block from the rooming house from about 4:00 until 6:00 o'clock. No Lupe!

Eduardo took a chance. He pulled his ball cap down low and put on sunglasses. He walked up to the rooming house office. Aunt Bessie was at her desk.

"May I help you?"

"I am looking for a room. What do you have?"

"You are lucky. A young lady just moved out. I have a small room in the back with one window. Would you like to see it?"

"Yes. Please," he followed her to the rear of the first floor."

"What do you think? Is it what you need?"

"No. I would like something a bit larger," he had noticed some strands of blond hair in the waste can. The room had not been cleaned yet, "I thank you for your kindness though. I will look some more."

To himself, "So Lupe has moved. I will find her," he drove back to the hospital.

Eduardo sat off-and-on for three days. He finally spotted her. An expensive older car picked her up. He followed carefully behind. The car turned west and soon drove by the edge of a golf course. It turned into a small street a few blocks later. The car went up a curved driveway and parked. A gray-blond haired man and the *rubia* got out. He recognized her from New York. Now he knew.

He dialed his cell phone, "Scippio, I found her. What do you want me to do?"

"Do what we talked about and get on back. I'm short handed and I need you. I have three of my *primo hombres* in jail."

Eduardo clicked OFF and drove to the warehouses along the river. He wanted to retrieve his pistol and some other items he had purchased. They were stored in the small shed he had rented two days ago. He parked the rental car in the shadows and walked back towards the high fence. He unlocked the shed door.

CHAPTER THIRTY-SIX

Tom Delano drove through the warehouse district. There had been some reports of trespassing and pilferage of small equipment in some of the small storage buildings. They had been doing this at random for five days. It was his turn to drive and the old sarge was carefully looking between the buildings as they drove slowly by. They had been cruising for two hours.

"Stop! I need to take a look back there. I can't see all the way to the end." Mike got out and walked back. He saw a dark green car parked in the shade. The sergeant walked a little further and saw a man unlocking a door.

He thought to himself, *he looks out of place wearing a tie and a nice sport jacket in this warm weather. And I'll bet that's a rental car.*

He saw the man pull the magazine back on a pistol and check it. The fellow put it back in a small holster and carried it to the car. He set it inside the trunk. Mike Strand, slipped out of sight around the corner of the building. He waited until the man turned to open the car door and then slipped across the road to the patrol car.

"Tom, pull up ahead and back in between the buildings and be really quiet."

Tom backed in, "What's going on Mike?"

"I don't know. I just have a gut feeling. He has a weapon. It's in the trunk. We'll follow this guy when he pulls out. Stay way back. I think he is from out of state. It's dusk, but don't turn your lights on." All the police cars had been re-wired to keep the lights from coming on automatically.

Eduardo pulled out onto the street between the main warehouses and headed for the river road. The sun was almost down—his headlights came on. Tom and Mike followed him carefully.

Eduardo followed the road along the golf course and turned down the small road. He parked under some trees and watched the big house where Lupe lived. Tom and Mike were backed into an access road watching. Eduardo didn't get out. The bag was still in the trunk.

And then he spotted the car, *I am being followed. Just like the cops in New York, but I know how to outsmart them—the Guardia.*

He waited about an hour and then slowly moved along the road. Evidently the two policemen were bored. They didn't realize he was gone for about four minutes—too late.

Eduardo circled around past the golf course and came in behind the big house on the next street. There were no alleys in this part of the city, but there was an empty lot. He parked the car on the opposite side of the street in the dark and carefully walked through the lot.

There was only a six-foot fence between the house where Lupe now lived and the lot. Eduardo was up and over the fence in less than a minute. He slowly moved about the grounds, using bushes and trees as cover. The house looked to be six years old. Some of the trees were very mature. They had been moved in and transplanted by the previous owner. He stayed in the shadows; there was now a half-moon.

As he neared the front, he looked out in the street, the cops were gone. He smiled.

Eduardo checked all of the windows carefully; he made no noise. One leaded glass style window on the west side was not like the rest. It must have been purchased later and installed. The latch was different on the inside. He figured he could open it with a small stainless steel wire that he always carried.

He carefully walked around to the front. The double doors could be forced open, but they would make a noise. On the east side he spotted it—a box. Express Security. The box was bolted to a chunk of concrete buried in the ground and the bolt heads were inside the box. He knelt behind the bushes and could just barely make out the hinge joints in the moonlight.

"This is not going to be easy. When I come, I'll have to bring a drillmotor." He had enough for the night. He peeked into the large room. There was a security panel on the far wall. A red light was on. It was armed. He walked slowly back, scaled the wall, and drove away; heading for his room.

CHAPTER THIRTY-SEVEN

Lupe could not tell if she was dreaming or not, *perhaps I should pinch myself.*

She leaned back against three pillows piled near the headboard on her bed. She looked around the room. It was hard to believe that she had lived in a small attic room in New York City not so long ago.

She clicked the remote control resting on the nightstand. The news came on.

The war in the Middle East was escalating; Lebanon and Israel. Lupe remembered her history, Spain had been under Muslim influence for six hundred years.

I wonder how it will all end, she clicked to a movie channel.

It was **El Cid** with Charlton Heston.

CHAPTER THIRTY-EIGHT

Eduardo drove to the airport and turned the Hertz car in. He hailed a taxi and was given the third one in line; "Take me to the Marriott please."

He rented another car at the Marriott, a dark brown Ford. Along the way he stopped at Home Depot and bought a portable drillmotor with cash. In the early hours of the next morning he drove to the same vacant lot. He parked under a tree and scanned the area. All of the homes about him were dark. He put out his cigarette and carefully opened the door—he had removed the fuses.

Donnie Kelly walked quietly down the sidewalk in the dark carrying his fishing pole and a small tackle box. This street frightened him on moonless nights. He was extra quiet when he was frightened. Tonight there was only a quarter-moon and lots of clouds. The light waned and waxed. Donnie hoped his buddy was ready. They were going to the river early and fish. They had a favorite spot and wanted to make sure nobody beat them to it.

As he neared the middle of the block at the vacant lot, he saw a dark car. A man got out and climbed over the fence. Donnie stopped. He had his dad's cell phone. He moved and watched, just barely peeking over the stone fence.

Karl had gone to bed at ten. He had been up twice. He didn't know how to set the alarm so he had ignored it. Something awakened him again and he got up and peeked out. It was a longtime habit, *was that a shadow or somebody moving?*

He watched the spot for a few seconds. It was human. A man was bent low to the ground and moving towards the side of the house. Karl couldn't see. He quickly went to the spare bedroom and looked down. The man seemed to be heading for the sliding doors on the east side. Karl grabbed his pants and shirt from his room and donned them.

Donnie saw the man head towards the side of the house. He hurried back and used his pocketknife to let the air out of one of the front tires by pressing the valve stem needle.

He called 911 and told the dispatcher.

They would send out a patrol car right away. He also told the dispatcher about letting out the air. The dispatcher had laughed.

Karl moved to the drapes at the side of the doors. There was a rasping sound and a small whir—then the door slid open. The clouds moved across the moon, he could see him. Karl slammed as hard as he could on the man's arm. There was a loud scream and a crunching sound. The fellow ran towards the fence! Karl yelled for him to stop!

A loud siren was close by. The man swiftly scaled the fence and ran to his car. He backed away and as he straightened out, he couldn't steer with a flat tire and only one arm—he smashed into a large tree.

The police threw a spotlight on him and yelled, "Police! Get out of the car with your hands raised. Very carefully!"

Eduardo did as he was told. One officer grabbed the keys and raised the trunk. There was a bag with extra ammo. There was some rope, a can of chloroform, and a roadmap of Dayton and Montgomery County. This house was ink marked with an X. The man was carrying a pistol and a hammer; he had left the drillmotor on the patio.

Tom Delano and the Sergeant pulled up in front of the house. They had been in the warehouse district again when they received the call—along with about six other patrol cars. Lupe and her grandmother were on the front steps when Tom pulled up.

The radio came on. A voice said, "We got him." The boy that called 911 said there was only one man."

"Be careful anyway until you are sure."

Tom asked, "Were you two here alone?"

"No. The little Swedish girl, Noora. She is asleep. Also a good friend of the family is here. I think upstairs. I will get him."

She came downstairs with a man close to her own age, "This is a good friend, Roberto Sanchez. He has come to visit and perhaps stay for a while."

Tom stuck out his hand, "Pleased to meet you. A guest eh. Where are you from?"

"I have lived in many places. I was born in New Mexico. I have heard of you from Lupe. She told me many things."

"I hope they were all good." The man only smiled.

The sergeant turned to Lupe, "The patrol car is here now. Lupe, see if you know this man. We are sure he is from out of State."

Lupe looked into the backseat, "I have seen him in New York. I think he works for Ladero."

"OK, run him downtown. We'll be there shortly. Tom come with me. We need to photograph the doors and the drill motor."

He turned towards the family, "Would you Mr. Sanchez and you Lupe, please come down to the station. We will need a statement and an identification. Officer Delano will bring you both back."

"I don't know his name, just that I have seen him in New York. Does Mr. Sanchez need to come along? He only slammed the door on the man's arm."

"I guess not. I'll just take his statement. Oh! By-the-way, Mr. Sanchez, did you have the alarm system on?"

"No. I don't know how to turn it on. Lupe does, but she was upstairs when I went to bed."

****

Lupe was watching from behind a one-way mirror. She was listening to the man being questioned.

"I think he is lying and he does know Scippio Ladero. He works for him, I am positive."

"Well, he won't be going to New York soon. We got him on several charges, breaking and entering, illegal firearms, and false insurance papers to be used with a rental car. He had them forged somewhere, probably in New York City. Also he has a false drivers license, a counterfeit VISA card, and there will be more things as we think of them. He'll get some time in one of our jails."

"Lupe, I'll take you home as soon as you sign this."

She looked up at Tom and smiled. She signed a statement declaring that she had seen the man in New York City and that she was positive he worked for Scippio Ladero and that she had seen them together several times.

Tom drove slowly; the sun was starting to come up, "How about breakfast? We have never had breakfast together."

"Yes. I am hungry. I would be getting up about now. I don't go in today until eleven because I have the late shift tonight."

"Great! I know a place that makes wonderful Dutch pancakes and they also have imported Dutch sausage."

"I have never had those,"

They left the little café an hour later and Tom drove her home, "Would you like to come in for a while? I don't need to get ready for work for a couple of hours."

"Sure," he sat in the easy chair in the den. Roberto Sanchez was already seated across the room by the fireplace. He had his slippers off and was sitting in his stocking feet.

Tom looked closely. The man had some of the features of Lupe's grandmother. He also somehow looked something like Lupe. And he was a blond. Always the cop, Tom had a thought.

"How do you like America?"

"Oh, I think it is...." he stopped short, "....this part is much different than New Mexico. It is partly a desert where I came from. There are trees in the mountains—and snow, but not like they are here along the river."

Tom knew that something was wrong. He would ask Lupe and he didn't think she could lie to him. They were getting closer.

Ileana brought them some coffee. Thomas watched her. She sat the cup and saucer next to Roberto, but did not give him a lover's glance. Not even like a friend. Took him for granted it seemed. It dawned on him, *this was the lost brother from Spain. But why the secrecy?* He wondered. He thought to himself again, *always a cop.*

They talked about the weather, Dayton, the police force, and what Roberto had worked at until he retired. Roberto was somewhat vague. It was a business, but Thomas was never quite sure what kind. It obviously paid well. He knew that Lupe and her grandmother had nothing. This house was a mansion. More questions to ask Lupe.

She came down the stairs, "Tom, can you drop me at the hospital please. I want to go in early. I have something to look up in the hospital medical library."

"Sure. Hey, how about dinner tonight? I know another great place."

"Alright, but I don't get off until almost midnight. Hey! I'm gaining weight."

"Midnight is fine. This place will stay open for me."

She gave him an odd look.

There was almost no traffic. Tom stopped by the emergency doors. As he clicked the door lock open he leaned over and kissed her, "See you before midnight."

At a few minutes before midnight, Tom was waiting. He had on a white shirt and tie.

"Why are you wearing a necktie. Should I go home and change clothes? What kind of a place is this?"

"So many questions. Just come as you are. I have been to a meeting."

Tom drove quickly away and was soon out into the farm country. After three or four miles, he stopped at a white painted farmhouse—the design was in the style of the 1920's. There was a long gravel drive with old trees lining each side. A barn, in good shape, could be seen in the headlights. There was a dog growling and the hair was raised on his backbone.

Tom got out first, shushed the dog, and opened the screen door on the side door for Lupe.

"Are you sure this is a restaurant?" Tom was silent as he took her arm. The dog flopped down on the porch.

Tom rang the doorbell, a man dressed neatly in a dark suit answered and invited them in. The dinning room table was set for four. A beautiful Damask linen tablecloth covered the large table. Shining silverware and delicate dinnerware and there were two large candles burning. The older man stood at the entrance to the kitchen.

"Tomas, there are four plates. Is there someone dinning with us?"

A pleasant looking gray-haired lady slipped off her apron as she entered the room and stood by the man. She had her best dress on.

"Lupe. I would like you to meet my grandparents, Mr. and Mrs. Delano; Edna and Arnold. Grandma and grandpa, this is Lupe."

"We have heard so much about you, please be seated."

"And I have heard so much of you, mostly on the train ride to New York. And thank you," Lupe sat at the chair Tom was proffering. Arnold Delano scooted one out for grandmother Edna.

She turned to Tom, "You are a rat. I should yell at you in Spanish—El Raton!" She turned to his grandparents, "….and you two are just as bad. He had me thinking we were going to a restaurant someplace." They all laughed.

It was a wonderful midnight dinner. Lupe seemed to have known the grandparents forever—and they liked her. Tom beamed.

Grandmother Delano started cleaning up the table, "Let me help." The two women were soon finished.

"Lupe, would you like to spend the night? We have an extra bedroom."

Lupe was tired. It had been a long day, "I think that would be nice. I am tired and my grandmother is used to me working odd hours. She will not think anything of my not coming home. Tomorrow I don't go into the hospital until late, like today—I mean yesterday," she laughed.

It was settled.

"Lupe, I have one more question before we go to bed. Roberto is really your uncle isn't he?"

She looked at him for a moment, "You already know don't you? Yes, he is. My grandmother has looked for so long. Are you going to say anything? He really just wants to live in peace."

"OK, I won't ask any questions about him. Your grandmother is wonderful. She deserves to know her brother. I suppose it is best for me to just forget it. Goodnight."

CHAPTER THIRTY-NINE

Scippio Ladero looked at the letter again. It was from the man in Ohio that he had hired to furnish the pistol and information on Lupe Guzman. The letter said that Eduardo had been arrested and he had pointed a finger at Scippio as a co-conspirator.

It is time for me to disappear for a while. I theenk Miami, he walked to his bedroom to pack.

Forget the rubia, she is no coming back to New York anyway an I can't no get my guys out of jail. Gotta save myself, he locked the door, walked down the stairs, and caught a cab to Penn Station, *I will be in Florida mañana noches; the train runs to a spur line connection to Washington DC and then all night to Miami.* He had checked the time schedule many times the last few years. He paid the cabbie and hurried. The train left in just a few minutes. He would pay premium for a seat, but he didn't care.

****

"Tomas, I want a traditional wedding. I would like a nice, but simple wedding gown, readings from the Scripture, a Psalm, homily, nuptials, introductory, and the Eucharist; with a procession and music—a penitential. What do you want?"

"I am a traditionalist too. I like what you just said. I would like a reading from the New Testament as well."

"*Si,* that is traditional. Do you want a cantor for the Psalm?"

"No, just read it. Perhaps an Acclamation could be sung by a cantor."

"The Padre will ask us a couple questions about freedom of choice, faithfulness to each other, and the acceptance and upbringing of our children."

"How many children do you want?"

"Hey! You are not the Padre. Only he can ask."

"No, really. How many? Two, three, more maybe?"

"I want children, *Si*. We will see. Back to the cantor and Gospel reading. This will be the same as in New York. Only we do some of it in Spanish. Then we will exchange vows and our rings will be blessed and we exchange them at the last."

"Then the gifts and the singing—the preparation of the Altar. Then the prayer and Sanctus singing. And singing of the Great Amen."

"Wow! It seems like you have been to many weddings."

"Only four. I loved every one of them. Even the poor in New York City would manage to find money to dress for the occasion."

"Oh, and Agnus Dei at the end? And the final blessing. Ah! *Si*. It will be a wonderful wedding."

"Don't forget the kiss and recessional. I have only been to one wedding, but I remember the kissing part."

"Tomas, you are bad."

He bent her head a little and gave her a firm kiss. She looked at him a second and kissed him back. They strolled towards the car, both deep in thought.

"Tomas where will we live?"

"I have been living on the farm, but that won't do. My grandparents own ten acres down the road. Grandpa bought it years ago because it had a well on it. It is part of his pasture now. He doesn't run milch cows anymore. And I have already asked, they both said we could build a house on it. We just need to fence one side. There are still a few sheep and the four horses."

"That sounds wonderful. Who would have believed it? Six months ago I was living in an attic. Where will we ever get the money."

"The land is paid for."

He stopped for a moment. "Have you ever ridden a horse?"

"No, I have seen the New York police riding them. I'm afraid of them. The cops sometimes bump their horses into unruly crowds."

"Really! We don't have any horses here, but I have been riding horses since I was five years old. I love horses. I will have to teach you."

"You will be my *Caballero Blanca*—my white knight."

"Perhaps not, but I will start teaching you about horses as soon as we get back from our honeymoon."

The church was packed. There were people from the hospital, from the police department, some firemen and their wives, Aunt Bessie, and three others from Aunt Bessie's rooming house. There were several couples from his high school class and a great uncle, his grandmother's brother, who had driven down from Detroit.

The wedding went just as Lupe, her grandmother Ileana, and grandmother Delano had planned. Instead of rice, the guests threw wheat. Birds would eat the wheat, but not the rice. Nobody had to clean it up.

Noora had been the flower girl. She was still in the temporary custody of Lupe with the hospital administrator, Mr. Slade, being the actual custodian.

Ileana treated Noora like her own daughter. Nothing had been heard from the officials in Sweden and a lawyer in town, Francis Lopez Calderon, was arranging paperwork for the little girl. He specialized in obtaining paperwork for illegals from South America, so why not one from Sweden. It seemed almost certain that Noora would be able to stay in America.

A limo picked Thomas and Lupe up and drove them to the airport. They were honeymooning in Las Vegas. Tom had reserved a suite at the Venetian Hotel Casino and he had booked them First Class on American Airlines through Chicago and on to Las Vegas. On their fourth day he had booked two seats on Scenic Air for a flight over the Grand Canyon, they both wanted to see the giant hole in the earth.

The building contractor had obtained permits from the county and would level a house pad and start digging the half-basement for their new house before they flew back from Las Vegas.

"We will stay with grandmother and my uncle until the house is finished. How long do you think?"

"A month and a half, the contractor says. And as soon as we get back, I have to get back to work, I have no more days left, I've used them all."

"I want to play Wheel of Fortune. I have seen it on TV. It would be fun."

"Ok, but I'm playing poker."

EPILOGUE

Mikel rolled down the car window. The Padre was walking towards the cemetery, "Padre! I need to tell you something. I moved two tombstones. Carlos' stone is over a real body and the other stone is over the one filled with rocks. Before you leave the Church someday, Padre, you must move the stone markers back. It took three of us to move them one night."

"I understand Mikel. I will do that. I will be here another six years I am sure. How have you been?"

"Bueno Padre! Bueno! Things are going well. I also have something for you," he handed the Padre an envelope with US stamps on it. Mikel drove slowly away.

The Padre opened the envelope. There was no return address. Inside there was only a Swiss bank draft—a draft for fifteen thousand Euro-dollars, *ah. Carlos did not forget the children. So many letters from America in such a short time,* he tore the corner off with the stamps, he would save them along with the first ones. They were all different.

Mikel was headed for the plains. The last two missions were good. Tonight would be better. He reached into his pocket for his cell phone. This phone call would start it—they would be right on time. His men had put up detour signs a kilometer or so on each side of the two bridges.

Mikel dialed. A voice answered. Mikel said, "Euskadi Ta Askatasun—Basque Country and Liberty." He dialed the other number and said the same thing. The bridges would be gone within the hour.

He smiled and made a U-Turn. He had a date; a girl he had gone to college with was living in Toledo. Her husband had been killed in Iraq almost two years ago, *ah! It is a good deed to console a vidua, especially such a beautiful widow. It is almost a duty!* He smiled and thought, *Spain would be such a good place if they would just leave us alone.* Mikel repeated to himself, *Euskadi Ta Askatasun!*

Antonio Chion walked up to the barred window counter inside the pawnshop, "I have taken Sccippio Ladero's place. We will be bringing things in from time to time. You do not foresee a problem, yes?"

His cousin Jamie Aragon stood behind him, his right hand inside his jacket.

The fat owner was shaken; he could see a gun butt sticking out of Antonio's coat. There was also a big Spaniard, with a shaved head, standing by the exit door. He had his right hand inside his jacket pocket.

"No! No problem. I will be here."

Tonio smiled and backed out of the door. The three men walked away into the dark. The pawnbroker wiped his damp forehead with a monogrammed handkerchief, *I'm good for another month.*

ABOUT THE AUTHOR

F. Eugene Barber was born on a sharecrop farm in the Midwest at the start of the Great Depression and first attended a rural school with nine other students ranging from the first to the eighth grades. He trapped for furs, hunted, fished, worked on farms and ranches branding cattle, mending barbed wire fences, and vaccinating calves until joining the Air Force just after graduating from high school at age seventeen. During the Korean War, he was an engine mechanic for a short time on Pusan Airfield, Republic of Korea and then later, a Crew Chief and Line Chief in the 5th Field Maintenance, 9th Bomb Group, 15th Air Force, Strategic Air Command, Travis AFB on SAC's huge Atomic Bomb carrying B-36. After discharge in late December of 1952, the former Staff Sergeant used his GI Bill and earned an AS in engineering, a BA, and an MBA over a twenty-five year time span.

Mr. Barber has worked all over the world; North, South, and Central America, the UK, Scandinavia, Europe, Polynesia, Russia and Russian Siberia, Finland, South Africa, Red China, Korea (ROK), Japan, Australia, Turkey, Egypt, and Saudi Arabia. He and his wife lived for a time in Yorkshire, UK where he was part of the Status of Forces on a covert Spec Ops base. His favorite countries, after the USA, would be Australia and Canada.

Fred has worked in Aerospace, DOD, DOE, FAA, and the INTEL communities most of his working life and occasionally still consults on special projects. Some of Mr. Barber's tasks have been on the Airborne Laser Project (ABL) for three years at the Birk Flight Test Center, Edwards AFB, a year as a contract/consultant in Minnesota on large remotely controlled Navy guns, another year on a small covert base in the desolate Nevada Desert working with UAVs in the Special Projects Office, in Washington on a composite LearJet aircraft, and lastly lecturing on ISO9001 and AS9001 Quality Systems in ten major cities about the US—now after working sixty-five years, he finally retired. He and his wife of sixty-two years reside in Arizona within view of a beautiful desert lake—Lake Havasu.

Made in the USA
Las Vegas, NV
31 March 2022